Chenault looked up at Dumarest. "The ship on which you left Earth must have had more than a name. What were its markings?"

A device totally unfamiliar and now almost forgotten. One Dumarest drew with frowning slowness on the paper Chenault pushed toward him.

"This? Are you sure?" Chenault looked up from the paper, rising as Dumarest nodded. "Let me see, now." He moved to a shelf, took down a heavy volume bound in cracked and moldering leather, riffled through the pages to stand, finger on an item. He said, "The clue, Earl. You've given me the final clue. I know where Earth is to be found."

SYMBOL OF TERRA

E.C. Tubb

DAW BOOKS, INC.

DONALD A. WOLLHEIM, PUBLISHER

1633 Broadway, New York, NY 10019

First Printing, September 1984

1 2 3 4 5 6 7 8 9

PRINTED IN U.S.A.

Chapter One

Dumarest saw the movements as he made his way along the valley; small flickers of red which could have been the flirt of a scarlet wing, the nodding of a bloom, the glow of reflected sunlight from a gleaming leaf. Facile explanations and none of them true; a bird would have risen, there was no wind to stir a flower and the sunlight streamed high to leave the valley in shadow.

Halting, he plucked a leaf and chewed it as he studied the terrain. Above and before him, monstrous against the sky, the bulk of a mountain reared in rugged splendor its natural beauty now enhanced by the glowing colors of sunset. At its base time and weather had conspired to form a deep, wedge-shaped declivity, flanked with steep inclines fringed with shrubs and stunted trees; vege-

tation which swept down to soften the bleak out-
lines of dirt and stone and to cover the floor with
flowered sward.

An artifice of man; the ground had been carefully leveled and graded, the plants set with calculated design to form a haven of beauty in which
birds could dwell and exotic flowers fill the air
with their heavy perfume. Faint in the distance
came the tinkle of running water.

Dumarest threw down the pulped leaf, catching
another glimpse of red as he resumed his progress.
Higher this time, but on the same side of the
valley. An enemy or a watchful guardian but one
lacking experience in remaining hidden. Or one
who wanted to be seen so another could remain
invisible.

A possibility but he doubted it. The vegetation
was too still and his sharpened senses would have
warned him of lurking danger. Steadily he moved
on down the valley to where the sides closed in to
meet the rock of the mountain. A great door pierced
it, made of massive timbers now closed and firm.
Windows flanked it, rising high like a multitude of
dark and wary eyes. Above them the sunlight painted
swaths of ruby and gold, orange and amber, pink
and vibrant chrome.

"Hi there!" Dumarest lifted his voice in a shout.
"Is anyone at home?"

His words flattened against the rock to fade and
become lost in the tinkle of water coming from a
stream rilling to one side. A chain hung beside the
portal and he pulled it, hearing the faint tone of a

bell. Repeated as again he hauled on the links. Turning he saw again the flash of red, closer now, lower on the slope.

"Chenault?" Again he shouted. "I've come to see Tama Chenault!"

A clearing stood before the door, set with a bench, and he moved toward it after plucking a fruit from a bush. Steel glimmered as he lifted the knife from his boot, using the edge to remove the rind, laying the blade beside him on the bench.

Eating, apparently relaxed, he listened to the tinkle of water, the soft rustle of leaves, the faint murmur of insects. A bird rose with a whirr of wings behind and to his left. There was a soft, squashy sound as if a boot had trodden a fallen fruit. Silence and then, with sudden abruptness, the unmistakable sound of clicking metal.

Dumarest threw himself to one side, snatching at the knife, hitting the ground as a dull report filled the air. Rising, he turned, blade lifted, leaving his hand in a blur of shimmering light as he spotted his target. As it hit, the woman screamed.

She was tall, slim, her skin the color of sunkissed grain. The green of her dress hugged a symphony of curves lushed with mature perfection. Her eyes matched the hue of her gown. The color of her hair was one he would never forget.

"Easy." Dumarest was on her before she could move, one hand closing on her wrist. "You aren't hurt."

"I thought . . ." She swallowed. "I felt . . ."

Nothing but the shock of impact as the thrown

knife had knocked the weapon she'd used from her hands. That and the fear born of the ruthless savagery of his face. It lingered as he sheathed the knife and picked up the gun. It was crude, a simple affair of twin-barrels with a large bore, the hammer needing to be cocked before it could be fired. An antique, but one as deadly as a laser in the right hands with the right ammunition.

"Yours?"

"No. That is—"

"Chenault's?"

"He—" She broke off. "You're hurting my arm."

Dumarest released her, hefting the gun. "Try to run and I'll use this. Why did you want to kill me?"

"I didn't. The gun fires a harmless dart. It would just have made you sleep for a while." She frowned at his expression. "You don't believe me. Look for youself." She pointed to where a gaudy tuft of feathers stood in the grass beyond the bench. "That's what I shot at you. You can check it."

"There's an easier way." Dumarest lifted the gun and aimed it at her body. Deliberately he thumbed back the hammer. "Two barrels," he said. "Two charges. Let's see if they're both the same."

She watched, wide-eyed as he moved to place her between himself and the bench. A hand lifted to her mouth as he began to close his finger on the trigger but she made no other sign of fear. Not even when he fired.

"Well?"

Dumarest looked at the dart standing from the wood of the bench. Perhaps it was as harmless as she'd claimed or perhaps she'd only thought it to be harmless. The latter, he guessed, she hadn't flinched from the decisive test.

He said, "Did Chenault give you the gun?"

"Yes."

"Why? What were you supposed to do with it?"

"Sometimes there are predators. They come into the valley and hunt the creatures here. When they do I take care of them."

"And visitors?" Dumarest shrugged as she made no answer. It was prudent to be cautious on even the most civilized of worlds and, in the Burdinnion, few were that. "Were you born here on Lychen?"

"No."

"Where then? Solis?" A guess and a wrong one as the shake of her head signified. "It's just that you remind me of someone I knew once. She had the same color hair as your own."

A red which burned in his heart like a flame. One which would never die as the memory of Kalin would never die. Kalin whom he had loved. Long gone now, the spirit which had won him dissipated, dead, leaving only the memory of a shape. Of eyes and hair and skin and mouth and . . . and . . .

And, suddenly, she was before him.

*　　*　　*

9

A bird broke the spell, rising with a thrum of pinions, leaves falling with a rustle—sounds of potential danger which jerked him from a dream. An illusion in which time had encapsulated and a person long gone was again at his side. Standing as she had so often stood before, looking up at his superior height, the long, clean line of her throat before his eyes, the magnet of her body, her chin, her lips, the flaming cascade of her hair. The emerald pools of her laughing eyes.

The hair, of course, it had to be the hair. The red which had betrayed her when she had watched him. That and her shape and her lips and her eyes. The eyes which held more than laughter.

She said, "Are you well?"

"Yes. Why do you ask?"

"You seem disturbed. Would you like to sit?" She gestured toward the bench. "Would you like some fruit? Water? I could fetch it from the stream."

And vanish while getting it but Dumarest felt certain she wouldn't. He watched as she crossed the clearing, noting the movement of her legs, the sway of her hips. A woman, but not the one he had known. Not the one he had imagined standing before him so short a while ago. Yet the impression had been so sharp. An illusion? The effect of the fruit he had eaten? Had the juice held a subtle hallucinogen which distorted reality?

He narrowed his eyes as she returned bearing water in some folded leaves. Against the vegetation she seemed neutral, a figure wearing green, one who could have been anyone—a female, well-made, but without character. An impression heightened by her face as she concentrated on her burden. It was smooth, somehow unformed, a collection of contours and planes. Then, as she noticed his interest, it firmed into what he had seen at first.

"Here." She handed him the folded leaf. "Drink and rest for a while."

Thirst and weariness made it easy to obey. The water was cool, refreshing, and Dumarest swallowed it all. Relaxing he smelt the perfume of the valley, listened to its quiet humming. The susurration of insects and growing things, the rustle of an upper breeze which stirred the vegetation as if to a giant's breath. Peace enfolded him and a calm tranquility.

To the woman he said, "What are you?"

"Who am I? My name is Govinda."

A question he hadn't asked and he wondered at the poetry which had made him liken her to some elemental spirit. One who lived in a tree or a stream, a thing of legend come real, belonging to this place like the stream and the plants, the enigmatic face of the house which was barred like a castle.

"Govinda." The name held music to match her tone. "Just that?"

"Isn't it enough?"

"Of course, but others I've known here on Lychen have several names."

"Nobles. Those aspiring to rank and position. They add names to each other like pearls." Her shrug dismissed the importance of labels. "And you?'' She smiled as he told her. "Earl Dumarest. I shall call you Earl. Were you born here on Lychen?''

"No more than you.'' He reached out and rested his fingers on her hand. The skin was soft and warm. "Which is your home world, Govinda?''

"I don't know.'' She met his eyes and answered the question she read there. "I had no real family and must have been passed around. I remember Yakimov. I did most of my growing there. After a while I moved to Kremer, then to Habralova then to other worlds. Finally I came here.''

"To stay with Chenault?''

"He looks after me, yes.'' She withdrew her hand from beneath his fingers. "What do you want with him?''

"To talk.''

"Just that?''

"Are you worried I'll hurt him? Is that why you tracked me and tried to knock me out?'' Dumarest shook his head and smiled. "You said he looked after you. I think it's the other way around. But why should he need looking after at all?''

She said, "You want to talk. What about?''

"I'll tell him that.''

"You can tell me and I'll tell him. Then, if he wants to see you, he will.''

"And if he doesn't?'' Dumarest let the question hang. "Surely he doesn't live here alone aside from you. There must be others.''

"There are.''

"In the house?''

"You talk too much, Earl, and say too little. Just what do you want with Chenault? To talk, you say, but how can I believe that?" She met his eyes, her own direct. "Why didn't you call ahead to arrange an interview? Why steal into the valley like a thief? How did you get here, anyway? I saw no raft."

"I walked."

"From where?"

Dumarest said, "That I'll tell Chenault when I meet him. And I'm going to stay here until I do. Tell him that and tell him we have mutual friends. Edelman Pryor for one. Tayu Shakira for another." He saw her face alter. "You know Shakira?"

"I—I'm not sure."

"Shakira of the circus of Chen Wei? You know him. Tell Chenault he sent me to him. Tell him now."

"I can't." She looked at the sunlight painting the mountain, the level of mounting darkness beneath it. The warning of approaching night which already filled the valley with dusty shadows. "Not yet but soon. I promise. You'll have to wait." Rising, she added. "If you want to leave do it now. If you see Tama and upset him you'll never leave this valley alive."

He came when the sun gilded the topmost peak of the mountain, turning the ice and snow which crusted it into an effulgent flame. Deceptive warmth. It would soon yield to the star-shot indifference of night. Dumarest heard the sigh as the great doors

13

swung open, and rose from the bench to stand facing it and the figure which came toward him, silhouetted against the light filling the hall.

"Dumarest? Earl Dumarest?"

"Chenault?"

He was tall, broad, thick around the waist. A man old as a tree grows old, as gnarled, as strong. The lines engraved on his face gave him a hard, emotionless appearance, one belied by his sudden smile, teeth flashing white between drawn-back lips. His eyes in their sunken sockets held a bright awareness.

"I'm Chenault. The girl said we had mutual friends."

"That's right."

"Edelman Pryor, for one." Chenault tilted his head a little, the thick mass of gray hair higher than Dumarest's own. "Tell me about him."

"Old, dry, dusty. He deals or dealt in old books, maps, logs, statuettes, legends."

"Statuettes?"

"He gave me one. A small thing he'd had for years. You may have seen it; a woman, grossly emphasized, of a size you could hold in a hand. He said it was the depiction of some ancient goddess. Erce."

"Mother Earth," said Chenault. "Or the Earth Mother. You have it with you?"

"No. Pryor is minding it for me. I didn't want to lose it."

"Neither did he." Chenault nodded, understanding. "You are subtle, Earl, I like that. A gift accepted and returned in a manner devoid of offense. He gave you my name?''

''Yes.''

''And Shakira?''

''Yes.'' Dumarest met the stare of the bright eyes, brighter now with reflected starlight. ''Tayu Shakira of the circus of Chen Wei. He said you could help me.''

''Tell me about him.'' Chenault listened as Dumarest obeyed. ''Did you know him well?''

''No.''

''But if he gave you my name—''

''No one knew him well,'' interrupted Dumarest. ''But if you knew him at all, really knew him, you must know one thing about him. He is—unusual.''

''In what way?'' Chenault leaned forward, tense. ''Tell me!''

Dumarest said, curtly, ''He is not like other men. He has hands sprouting from his waist. Extra hands.''

''The product of wild genes.'' Chenault sighed and relaxed. ''You know him. Tayu must have trusted you to allow you to live with that knowledge. Later you must tell me about him and also how you managed to make Edelman Pryor feel so indebted to you that he gave you his most prized possession. Govinda was right; you are a most unusual man, Earl Dumarest. I am proud to greet you as my guest.''

''It will be an honor to shelter beneath your roof.''

''The old courtesies.'' Chenault smiled his

pleasure. "It is good to hear the traditional words again. But I am remiss as a host. Govinda told me that you claimed to have walked here and must be fatigued. She was also curious as to where you came from. We are somewhat isolated here. The nearest village lies over a hundred miles to the west. The town—"

"I had a raft," said Dumarest, "but I didn't want to be followed. So I dumped it and came here on foot. From the other side of the mountain."

"Where water is scarce and game even scarcer. Well, you are here now, and can have all you need." Chenault gestured toward the open doors. "Shall we go in?"

The hall matched the barbaric splendor of the great doors; a place of vast dimensions, the roof peaked, the floor tessellated in garish diamonds of red and green. Colors repeated on the walls together with others of smoldering vividness set in a profusion of designs which Dumarest found vaguely familiar. As the doors closed behind them the air seemed to vibrate and the designs to blur, to seem to move as perspective changed, to freeze in a series of grotesque parodies.

Faces distorted by the painted masks peculiar to clowns.

A circus!

Dumarest halted as he recognized the vague familiarity for what it was. The floor, the hall, the peaked roof which depicted the summit of a tent, the designs themselves all reflections of a small and bizarre world. Now he could recognize the semblance of cages, the hint of watching beasts, the shape of a ring, the tiered seats, the hanging strands of a trapeze. An illusion created with paint and light and undoubted genius.

"You noticed." Chenault stood facing Dumarest his bright eyes direct. "What do you see?"

"A circus tent, of course. But—"

"Lopakhin created it. He felt the need and I permitted it. Tyner is a genius and, I suppose, I have a weakness for the grandiose. A happy combination and one which allows of such indulgences. Others also find it amusing and, at times, they come to stare and gawk and make their observations. Fools for the most part, but it does no harm to cater to their whims as long as they do not clash with my desires." Casually Chenault added, "Perhaps you have met those I'm talking about. Jaded dilettantes from the great Houses. Those of influence and position with too little to do and too much time in which to do it. At times they visit me and request permission to view my hall. Sometimes I accommodate them."

"You are gracious."

"Sensible. Why arouse antagonism when there is no need?" Chenault turned and moved down the hall. As Dumarest fell into step beside him he said, "I give a little and receive much in return. If they think I am an amusing eccentric then that is to my advantage. Also, from such people, information can be gained."

As to his own presence on Lychen and what had happened since he had landed. Dumarest glanced at his host and wondered just how much the man knew and what he intended. An academic question; if the information he had gathered was true then he had no choice but to stay close to the man until he had gained the coordinates of Earth. The secret Chenault owned—or did he?

Always there was doubt and there had been too many disappointments and yet, this time, Dumarest felt close to success. A conviction based on instinct but which he knew could be contaminated by hope. And if this was another blind lead it would be best to discover the truth without waste of time.

Dumarest said, bluntly, "Shakira gave me your name and that of this world. He said you would help me."

"Of course. And I shall."

"Then it might help if I told you what I'm looking for and—"

"But later." Chenault halted as they reached the end of the hall. "There is a time and place for all things and welcome guests are too rare to be hurried. You are in need of food and rest and other comforts. Later we shall talk." The clap of his hands created echoes which murmured to silence. As they faded, a man appeared, standing, waiting, in the age-old attitude of one who served. "Baglioni," said Chenault. "He will guide you to your room and attend you. Until later, my friend."

A wave and he was gone leaving Dumarest with his guide. Baglioni was small; a man with the body of a child but with the face of an old man. A midget who bowed and gestured for Dumarest to follow as he stepped to a wall. He froze as Dumarest dropped a hand on his shoulder.

"Can you hear?"

"Yes, my lord."

"And speak too, so I see. Are there many like you in this place?" He smiled as the man remained silent. "Would money persuade you to find your tongue? No? I thought not. Your master is fortunate in having so devoted a servant." Without change of tone Dumarest added, "When did you leave the circus?"

"My lord?"

"What were you? Acrobat? Tumbler? Clown?" Pausing, he added, "Or were you in a sideshow with the rest?"

Baglioni was stiff. "I don't understand what you mean, my lord. Now, if you will follow me, I will guide you to your room."

Chapter Two

Bizarre luxury everywhere, the walls painted in striations of complementary colors, the furnishings adorned with grotesque carvings depicting men and beasts and things of the sea and air. The bed was wide, soft, the woven cover resembling an ancient tapestry. The bathroom adjoining was bright with mirrors and gilded metalwork.

Dumarest stripped and stood beneath the shower, washing away the sweat and grime of his journey with blasts of hot and icy water, foaming unguents and cleansing soap. With a sponge he tended to his clothing, removing dirt and stains from the neutral gray plastic. Dried, naked aside from a towel wrapped around his waist, he padded into the bedroom and moved toward the window.

He had seen this window from below, a round

eye which gave a view of the valley, set, he guessed, to one side of the great doors and high in the cliff. The pane was immovable to his touch, locked or sealed to the frame; even if broken it would give only to the sheer face of the cliff. If the door to the room should be locked from the outside it would become a prison despite its luxury.

A fact assessed and dismissed; if Chenault intended him harm the danger lay in the man himself and not the furnishings of his house. Leaning forward Dumarest studied the terrain below. The valley was dark now, filled with gloom alleviated only by the starlight which touched trees and shrubs with a silver glow. A wrongness; the windows should be streaming light unless the glass had been treated to blank it from within. That explained their dark and empty appearance from outside and he wondered how many had watched his progress down the valley.

Turning, he made for the switch and killed the interior illumination. The window, now filled with the silver glow of starlight, painted the chamber with a ghostly luminescence.

One broken by a warm fan of brilliance as the door opened and Govinda stepped into the room.

"Earl?" She had not expected the dimness and drew in her breath as she saw him move. "Oh, there you are."

The door closed behind her and she stepped toward him, her hair black in the pigment-robbing light. Her gown was formal, high at the neck, covering her arms, falling to just above her feet.

Around her the air was heavy with the scent of flowers.

"It's beautiful, isn't it?" She gestured toward the window. "It can be darkened if the light bothers you. See?" At her touch the round eye grew dim and finally dark. "You need only turn the control. One way for total darkness the other for as it was." The room grew palely bright again as she demonstrated. "I came to see if there was anything you needed."

"That was kind."

"Tama likes his guests to be comfortable."

"Is it your job to see they are?"

"I don't want you to miss anything. Look!" She pointed at the window. "See?"

Beyond the pane, in the valley, came a sudden dart of brilliance. It was joined by another, more, and within seconds the area was filled with a host of scintillant streaks of burning colors which moved and died as quickly as they had appeared.

"Firebirds," she explained. "They rest and eat and glow as they fly."

Nocturnal creatures and there could be others yielding equal pleasure. Dumarest turned as the woman pressed close beside him, her face and eyes turned toward the view outside. In the pale light her face looked oddly different from what he remembered, even more unformed than it had when she returned with the water. A nondescript combination of basic features, older, betraying lines which should not have been missing. Then, conscious of his examination, she turned to face him and, at once, was younger, more alive.

"Earl." Her hand rose to touch him, long fingers resting on his naked shoulder, falling to move over the pattern of scars on his torso. A gentle touch which lingered, then, reluctantly, fell away. "Dinner will be soon," she said. "You'll find clothing in the cabinet."

"My own will do."

"Not at the table of Tama Chenault. Dinner here is a festive occasion and he has a high regard for what is proper. Please, Earl." Her hand rose to touch him again. "Is it so hard to accommodate an old man?"

The clothing was black edged with gold, the blouse fitting close to match the smooth fit of the pants. Garb to be expected in the great houses where formality was the rule. Dressed, Dumarest looked at himself in the mirror; a tall, wide-shouldered man, the bulk of his torso diminishing to a flat stomach, a narrow waist.

"It fits, Earl, and it suits you." Standing beside him, framed in the mirror, Govinda stared at him with emerald eyes. In the restored lighting of the room her hair burned with a ruby splendor. She too wore black, the skirt banded with gold, her costume complementary to his own. "You look a warrior. A king."

"And you look a queen, my lady."

"Your lady, Earl?" In the mirror her face seemed to blur as if the glass had fogged; then, as he turned to face her, it was firm again. "That would

23

be nice if true. A pleasure but one coupled with pain. How could any woman ever be sure of you?'' Her laughter dismissed the question as it eased the moment. The muted throb of a gong echoed through the room. ''The first warning, Earl.''

''Warning?''

''That dinner will soon be served. There will be two others. On the last the doors will be shut and if you aren't present you'll be denied a meal and thrown from the house.'' Her tone was light but he guessed she wasn't joking. ''Come.'' She slipped her arm through his. ''Let me show you the hall.''

A place he had seen but, entering it, he found it altered. The circus depiction had vanished and in its place loomed the brooding magnificence of a cathedral. A vista of soaring columns and arched roofs, groined, carved, set with the smoldering grandeur of stained glass windows. An illusion as had been the circus.

''It changes,'' said Govinda. ''Something to do with various pigments reacting to different forms of light. At one time you see this and at another, something else.'' She watched the movement of his eyes. ''You're impressed?''

Dumarest nodded.

''Tyner will like that. He's proud. If you want to make a friend just tell him how clever he is.''

Lopakhin was a squat barrel of a man with a twisted, cynical mouth and hot, restless eyes. He wore vivid hues in a jarring assembly; a garment which could have been taken as a mockery of rigid formality and an affront to his host. One Chenault chose to ignore and Dumarest guessed that the mode of dress was a part of the artist's facade. The mask he wore to cover an inward uncertainty. One augmented by an abrasive and arrogant manner.

"Hail to our visitor!" He rose from his place at the table, goblet in hand, bowing as Govinda led Dumarest into the room. "A brave man who has faced many dangers—and who has yet to face many more."

"Sit down, Tyner." The woman at his side matched him for bulk but her eyes held a patient understanding and her tone was gentle. Her dress was similar to that worn by Govinda, lavender instead of black with silver adornment instead of gold. Differences of no significance when compared to her face which was one mass of intricate tattooing. "Sit," she snapped when the artist hesitated. "You fail to amuse."

"And that, my dear Hilary, is the most heinous crime of all." Lopakhin shrugged and lifted his goblet, drinking, setting it down with a bang as he dropped into his chair. "To be serious. To regard life as something other than a game. Yet, to look at you—"

"Is to see beauty," said Dumarest quickly. "To witness the work of a master of his craft. My lady." He stepped forward and took the woman's hand, lifting it to his lips as his eyes searched her face. "Some are as nature intended," he said. "Many work to gain beauty. A few have it thrust upon them. I know worlds where you would be hailed as the epitome of femininity.''

"So my father often told me.'' Her voice held the echo of resentment. "I have yet to find one.''

"Beretae,'' said Dumarest. "Sunyasha. On both body-decoration is an art and unadorned flesh is held in small regard. Your presence graces this table.'' He turned to Lopakhin. "As does yours, my lord. The hall is a work of genius. I tell you it as others must have done. As more undoubtedly will.'' He reached for a goblet and lifted it. "I salute you!''

"That was well done,'' said Govinda as Dumarest took his place at her side. "Perhaps too well done.''

"No.'' The man facing her was lean, hard, his skin the color of ebony, his hair a close-knit mass of jetlike wool. "Ian Massak,'' he said. "I know your name and now I know you've brains as well as guts. A happy combination.'' To the woman he said, "If you're going to flatter anyone, Govinda, don't use half-measures. Go all the way whether it's to be cruel or kind.''

"And he knows how to be kind.'' The man at Dumarest's side nodded toward the tattooed woman. "Look at Hilary, I haven't seen her so relaxed for weeks.''

She was leaning back, smiling, happy as were the others at the table and Dumarest wondered if he'd passed a test of some kind. They had been the last to arrive, a thing Govinda could have managed, and Lopakhin could have acted as he had as part of a charade.

"I'm Toetzer." The man at Dumarest's side smiled a welcome. "Good to have you with us. That's Shior down there, next to him is Vosper, and—" He broke off as a bell chimed. "Later," he said. "Tama is about to give the blessing."

A hush fell as the echoes of the bell faded into a silence that lasted as, at the head of the board, Chenault sat as if carved from stone. A posture adopted by the others as Dumarest noticed with rapid movements of his eyes. One broken as Chenault moved, hands lifting, the left held stiffly upright before him, the palm to his right, the right hand also stiff lowering to rest on the tips of the fingers to form an unmistakable T.

Sonorously he said, "The one became the many and the many shall again become the one. This in the fullness of time."

A rustle around the table as the gesture was repeated and Dumarest was conscious of the scrutiny of a dozen pairs of eyes. A moment in which to make a decision and hope he offended none by following their example. As his hands came to rest Chenault said, "We ask the Mother to grant us strength. To give us aid. To guide our path. To favor us as her children. To her our devotion. Until the end of time."

A whisper like the rustling of leaves as the response echoed over the table. One in which Dumarest joined.

"Until the end of time."

Then, beside him, Govinda dropped her hands as did the others following Chenault's lead. For a

27

moment the solemnity of the moment lasted, then dissolved as doors opened and servants came to lift the covers from steaming dishes, to place new flagons on the table, to bring in a choice of meats and fish and vegetables flavored with a host of herbs and spices, cut and set to form elaborate patterns.

"Here!" Massak leaned forward, his knife extended, a morsel stuck on the point. "To you, my friend."

A ritual Dumarest recognized and which told him something of the man. He leaned toward the proffered morsel, took it between his teeth, used his own knife to spear a fragment and to offer it in turn.

"Peace and brotherhood," he said. "Wars without killing but, if killing there must be, let it be quick and clean."

The talk of mercenaries who had met after peace had removed the reason for their antagonism. The proffered morsel a sign of friendship, the taking of it a sign of trust.

Massak beamed as his teeth closed to scrape on the blade.

"Look after him, Govinda," he boomed. "If you don't then I will."

"But not in the same way, eh?" Lopakhin smirked as he reached for his wine. "But as good as, perhaps? I've heard of you mercenaries and what is it they say? Any port is—"

"Shut up, you fool!" Hilary was sharp. "Some things you don't joke about."

"Was I joking?" Lopakhin shrugged. "Well, let us talk of other things. Of long journeys, perhaps. Of other worlds. Of dreams and hopes and legends. Of children you yearn to go back home to. Home!" He hid his face in his goblet, droplets dewing his lips as he set it down. "Home—another name for hell especially when you're a child. Take Hilary, for example, held down, screaming, while her devoted father drove his needles into her face and body. Turned into a spectacle to titillate the rich and idle. Robbed of her dignity. Forced to sit nude while men goggled and wanted to do more than just look. Why should she ever want to go back home? Why should you?" His eyes met Dumarest's. "Why should anyone?"

"Sometimes they have pleasant memories." Toetzer selected a fruit and peeled it with thin, delicate fingers. "My home world was a kind place with soft winds and purple clouds and, at night, the stars formed patterns like faces with smiling eyes. We grew all we needed and helped each other and had fun at festivals and weddings and even at funerals. A life well-lived is no cause for grief. Why mourn someone who has moved on to better things? Do we begrudge a child a better way of life?"

"Paradise." Massak speared more meat. "But how real was it? Aside from your memories, I mean."

"It was real."

"Then why leave it?"

"Slavers." Toetzer's hands began to tremble.

29

E. C. Tubb

"They came and they took me. Others too, no doubt, but I can be sure only of myself. They sold me and I was—changed." The tremble had increased, the fruit falling from his fingers to roll on the table as he slammed his hands to the board. "Defiled," he whispered. "Degraded. Demeaned—God, why did it happen?"

Govinda said, "But why didn't you go back? When you had the chance, I mean."

"I couldn't. It wouldn't have been the same. I'd changed and . . . and . . ." Toetzer shook his head. "No. I couldn't go back."

"Of course you couldn't." Lopakhin was emphatic. "Your own good sense wouldn't let you. A man must be a fool to walk with his head turned to look over his shoulder at the past. No one wants to go back to their home world after they've left it. No one!"

He was wrong. Dumarest wanted nothing more.

The meal ended, servants clearing away the dishes, replacing them with others holding comfits, sweetmeats, tasty morsels designed to pique the senses rather than assuage hunger. Tisanes joined the wines, smoking pots containing herbal teas, others redolent of coffee, of chardle, of rich, thick chocolate.

Govinda said, "You can leave if you want, Earl. Or move around. Dance if you choose." Her eyes were inviting as the soft sounds of music stirred the air. "Or just sit and talk. Change places if you like. Would you care to talk to Toyanna?"

"Later, perhaps."

She was a lean and hungry-looking woman with a roach of silver hair and hands resembling claws. She reminded him of a harpy; a creature of carnival who urged clients to chance their luck or test their skills, knowing they had no chance. He wondered what Chenault saw in her and glanced to where he sat. He seemed asleep and had taken little part in the conversation but his eyes were open, bright in the light, slick with a watchful sheen. As Dumarest watched Baglioni came to whisper into his master's ear.

"No!" Chenault shook his head. "I will not be disturbed."

Again the midget spoke, his voice too low to hear.

"Tell them to go. It is not convenient. This is my house and I am its master. No!" His hand lifted to quench Baglioni's fresh appeal. "I don't care who they are. Send them away."

"Visitors." Massak shrugged as the midget scurried from the hall. "They picked a bad time but since when have the rich ever been considerate?" He turned toward Lopakhin, teeth flashing in a smile. "A pity, Tyner. They would have gawped at your hall and complimented you on your artistic merit and even offered you rich commissions to create for them a similar toy. I often wonder why you always refuse them."

"They could not appreciate my art."

"True, but the money is tempting."

"Money isn't everything. As you said, to them

31

such a creation would be nothing more than an amusing toy. I am not interested in entertaining fools." Lopakhin reached for a sweetmeat, bit into it, spat as an unexpected flavor filled his mouth. "Damn the thing! One day I'll have a word with the chef."

"His creations match life," said Massak. "Both are full of surprises. As an artist yourself you should appreciate his skill. For me such things are too subtle. I prefer simpler fare." He swept a space clear before him and set his elbow on the board, forearm lifted, hand spread and empty. To Dumarest he said, "Come, my friend, let us play a familiar game."

Dumarest shook his head.

"No flames," urged Massak. "No bowls of acid. No spikes or naked blades. Just a friendly test of skill and strength. The one who forces the other's hand to the table wins a promise."

"Such as?" Dumarest smiled as the other shrugged. "No. You would win and I'd be in your debt. In any case to gamble for unknown stakes is to wander blindfolded in a mine field. No man wants a friend to do that."

"True " Massak looked at the artist. "How about you, Tyner? No? Vosper?" He called down the table. "Shior?"

Dumarest rose and left the board to wander around the chamber. Alcoves held objects of delicate construction and obvious worth; vases, bowls, statuettes, jeweled flowers, insects fashioned from glinting metal. A polished plaque held the shadowy impression of a face tormented by endless suffering. One which moved as Dumarest leaned toward it. A mirror? A cunning work of art which took a basic reflection and augmented it with previously delineated lines?

"One of Lopakhin's creations." Toyanna stood beside him, the sheen of her silver hair making a brighter spot on the plaque. "He's crude and coarse and drinks too much but there's magic in him. As I think there is in you, Earl. Give me your hand."

"A reading?"

"You mock?" For a moment anger shone in her eyes then, smiling, she shrugged. "I forgot. A man like you needs always to be cautious but I mean you no harm."

"And can do little good." Dumarest was blunt. "The past I know and the future can take care of itself. I've no wish to listen to mumbled warnings of dire events which might or might not happen. Things never specified but only hinted at. Thank you for the offer, my lady, but this isn't carnival and I'm no gull."

"You think you know my trade?"

"I can guess."

"Because I asked for your hand?" She held out her own. "Take it. Does that make you a reader of palms?"

There was strength in the hand despite its thinness, matching the lithe grace of her body, the near-gaunt appearance of her face. Things Dumarest noted as he saw her eyes, watchful, sharp with calculation. A woman, he guessed, who had never been young but always too adult for her years. A trait which rarely yielded happiness.

His fingers touched her flesh, traced lines, paused as he frowned, moved on as, nodding, he released his breath.

"Your past is filled with shadows, my lady. Times of distress and hardship when, too often, you had to suffer the unthinking folly of others. None appreciated your sensitivity and you were hurt by their indifference. You have known rejection, scorn, contempt, anger. Often you have been misunderstood and the love you hold within you cries for recognition."

She said, dryly, "But it will come together with the man of my dreams. There will be recognition of worth and wealth and a long journey. A good try, Earl, but there could have been more detail. No reading should be too fast. You needed to pause, to ask questions in a casual manner, to incorporate the answers in later remarks. Yet, if you were put to it, you would make out."

Smiling, he released her hand. "Is that your professional opinion?"

"Hardly that." She returned his smile. "Hilary is the expert."

"But you've worked carnival?"

"As a healer, yes." She drew in her breath and met his eyes. "Herbs, unguents, lotions, philtres, tablets, pills; all harmless and most useless but the advice was something else. As was the treatment I gave at times. I had the knack for it. I could look at a client and tell if all was well. Sometimes I could be precise as to what was wrong and even take steps to cure it. Certainly I could warn against it. Do you believe that coming events can cast their shadow before them?''

"Fortune telling?"

"A man has a tumor growing in his brain. The signs are there for those with the skill to see. To state that, shortly, he will go mad and die is not to guess at the future but to know it. To be certain of it. The coming event has cast its shadow. You see?''

Dumarest nodded. "Do you still sell pills?"

"Not exactly but I do prescribe them when necessary." Her eyes held the dancing glints of amusement. "We should have been introduced, Earl. I am Pia Toyanna, Doctor of Medicine, Doctor of Psychology, of Radionic Healing and Psionic Manipulation." She added, casually, "I'm also a surgeon.''

One who had made Dumarest foolish. He admitted it and she shook her head, smiling.

"No, Earl, you made a wrong conclusion but it wasn't so far out. Now, may I take your hand?" She held it clasped in her own, not looking at him, her eyes half-closed as if she strained to see things beyond the normal range of vision. Then, sighing, she released his hand. "Strong," she said. "In you there is an incredible determination to survive. I guessed as much when I learned you were coming and—"

"You knew I was coming here?"

"Yes." She recoiled a little from the savage

35

intensity of his stare. "Yes, I did, a day or two ago."

"How?"

"I was told. Tama told me. It was after visitors had come and they had talked and he told me the news. About you coming and the deaths of the Karroum. They were full of it." Her eyes widened a little as she looked into his own. "Did you have anything to do with it, Earl? Is that why you chose to walk from the other side of the mountain?"

"Did Chenault tell you that too?"

"Of course. Me and others—we've been expecting you. But did you have anything to do with the deaths of the Karroum?"

He said, tightly, "Why ask? If you know so much you know the answer to that too. Anyway, what does it matter?"

"It matters." She was bleak. "The rule of the Karroum falls to Mirza Annette. A bitch, Earl. One who believes in revenge."

Chapter Three

In her was steel, granite, the biting chill of winter ice. Things Vaclav recognized as she was ushered into his office to stand glowering before his desk. A tall, broad-shouldered woman in her late middle age, her graying hair cut short to frame a harsh, uncompromising face. Her eyes, palely blue, were sunken beneath thick brows. Her nose was a jutting promontory dominating a thin-lipped mouth. Her hands, her chin, the column of her throat belied the femininity of breasts, hips and buttocks.

Without preamble she snapped, "You know who I am?"

"Of course." Vaclav gestured to a chair and waited until she had settled herself. "It is an honor to meet the Lady Mirza Annette Karroum."

"You know why I'm here?"

E. C. Tubb

"To inquire about the unfortunate incident which took place at the Crystal Falls. I assure you that, as Chief Guardian of Lychen, I made the most thorough investigation. Would you care for some refreshment? Tisane? Coffee? Wine?"

"Coffee."

"With brandy?" He reached for the intercom as she shook her head and gave the order. "While we are waiting, my lady, allow me to offer my condolences on the recent loss your House has suffered. The seventh lord was too young to die."

"When is too young?" Impatient anger edged her voice. "Hedren Anao Nossak was a fool. It would have been better for all had he died at birth. As it was he lived long enough to display his weakness, and his death has caused me serious inconvenience. Alone that was nothing but his uncle died with him and I have been forced to take on the leadership of the House of Karroum. As such I have a duty. None may harm a Karroum and escape the penalty."

"I understand, my lady."

"Do you?" Her tone held contempt. "I doubt it. Honor is instilled with the mother's milk, not adopted in later years to be worn as a garment. One too easily set aside for the sake of compromise or expediency. I'm sick of hearing such words. The path of honor is clear-cut, direct, inarguable. A life for a life! A hurt for a hurt! The creed of the Karroum and, by God, while I rule we'll abide by it!"

A fanatic and a dangerous one. Vaclav wondered what she had been doing in her years away from Lychen. Farming somewhere on a hostile world, he guessed, in the Burdinnion such were plentiful. Now, looking at her, sensing the stubborn pride radiating from her, he wished she had stayed away.

"My lady, you must understand that I can only work within the framework of the law."

"I want facts, Vaclav. Not excuses."

"Yes, my lady."

The coffee arrived and she drank it while he gave her what she wanted. He was patient. Old as she might be and intransigent as she undoubtedly was yet she had the power to break him and they both knew it.

She said, as he ended, "So Angado Nossak returned to this world with a man he'd met on his travels. One we know to be Earl Dumarest. He shared Angado's apartment at the falls. Some time later Angado was found dead in the main salon, his uncle Perotto with him, also dead, the room empty but for an injured cyber. And Dumarest?" China clashed as she set down the cup and saucer. "Gone. Running from the scene of the crime in a stolen raft. Is he guilty?"

"Of what, my lady?"

"The murders, what else?"

Vaclav said, "Angado was killed by a dart from the ring-gun his uncle was wearing. The same weapon caused Perotto's death. Cyber Avro was not injured but incapacitated by illness. The only other man in the apartment, a guard knocked out by Dumarest, was not present when the incident took place.''

"But Dumarest was. Together with a woman.''

"Wynne Tewson. The guard recognized her. Dumarest used her raft.''

"To escape.'' Mirza was curt. "From whom and for why? Innocent men do not run. He must have killed in that room. He certainly killed those in the other raft which followed him.''

"An accident. I have depositions. Three eye-witness accounts. The rafts were close and must have collided over the falls. Dumarest managed to reach safety by the use of auxiliary burners. He was fortunate.''

"You think so?''

"My lady?'' Vaclav sensed he was on danger-ous ground. Mildly he said, "He could have fol-lowed the others into the falls. His raft could have veered, spun, tilted, anything. He was lucky it didn't.''

"Is that why you haven't arrested him? I can't understand why he wasn't held for questioning. It seems to me that you have failed in your duty. To have ignored such an elementary precaution smacks of the most arrant stupidity.''

Vaclav looked down at his hands and fought to remain calm. A victory gained at cost—later he would pay for resisting the impulse to tell the bitch what he thought of her and her arrogant manner.

"My lady, you asked for the facts and have been given them. If you find them not to your liking I am not to blame. I am concerned with guilt, not revenge. With proof, not assumptions. As things stand there is no evidence against Dumarest.''

''But—''

''The incident over the falls was an accident, as three witnesses are willing to swear. There is no case to answer. The raft he used could have been stolen, true, but as the owner is dead there can be no complaint. The dart which killed Angado was fired from the ring worn by his uncle, as the evidence makes plain.''

''Evidence can be manufactured.''

''My lady?''

She was brutal in her curtness. ''Use your brains, man. Perotto's body showed extensive bruising. Injuries which could have been caused by savage blows. He could have been beaten helpless, his ring used against Angado and then turned on himself. Can you deny the possibility?''

''No, but where is the motive?''

''Did he need one? Perhaps Dumarest had outstayed his welcome. He could have thought to use blackmail against Angado and Perotto challenged him. He may have tried to steal.'' She made an impatient gesture. ''Do the details matter? Interrogation would have revealed the truth but you failed to hold him. More proof of your inadequacy.''

Vaclav said, stiffly, ''He was in a raft, my lady. It headed into the sky and was gone long before the guardians learned of the situation. I put out a routine trace but nothing was found. It could be anywhere.''

"Find it. Use every man and machine you have. I want it located. The raft and the man who used it. Understand?"

"I'll do my best."

"You'll do more than that—you'll find Dumarest." She drew in her breath then continued, in a milder tone, "As a girl I studied logic. You've supplied the facts as to what was found in that room and I've given an explanation to account for them. One you don't seem to like. Let's look at your idea. Angado killed by a dart from Perotto's ring. A fact beyond dispute. But what then? Suicide?"

"A possibility, my lady."

"Rubbish! If you believe that, you're a bigger fool than I take you for. With Angado dead Perotto had everything to live for." Her voice rose a little, the former mildness forgotten. "He was scum and may have deserved to die but he was of the Karroum and the one who took his life will pay. I swear it!"

The place held the stench she had hated since childhood; an odor of fear, pain, regret, terror. One compounded by the smell of antiseptics, bandages, drips, the sterilizing fluids used to treat the bedding and gowns. Like a prison, a hospital was a world unto itself where values changed and small things took on a tremendous import. As small officials regarded themselves as greater than they were.

"Aside!" The official wilted beneath her glare. "Where can I find Cyber Avro?"

"My lady." He didn't know her but her arrogance betrayed her class. "Please, my lady, if you will be so good as to wait." He gestured with the hand with which he had tried to bar her progress, pointing at a waiting room fitted with hard chairs, dusty walls, faded prints of scenes and men long dead. "I will summon Doctor Kooga."

"You will send him to me," she corrected. "Now direct me to the cyber."

He lay on a bed in a room containing the most expensive equipment the hospital could provide. As the room held the most comfort; things lost on the patient, who rested supine, eyes closed, his head swathed in an elaborate dressing. Beneath the covers his body looked like that of a man in the last stages of deprivation; the stomach concave, the torso a slight mound, the thighs like sticks, the arms resting above the material the same. What she could see of the face reminded her of a skull.

"My lady, I beg you!" Vaclav, beside her, betrayed the conflict which tore at his equanimity. "This is madness! He is of the Cyclan!"

"He was in the room."

"True, but he saw nothing. He was almost co-matose when we found him and needed emergency treatment. All this," his gesture embraced the room, the equipment, "is at the order of the Cyclan who have guaranteed to meet every expense. Kooga dropped all other cases to concentrate on this. He is working in close collaboration with Cyclan physicians." He added, as if in justification, "They communicate by radio. If they were present we wouldn't have this problem."

Nor the witness and Mirza drew in her breath as she thought about it. Vaclav had said nothing, her own intelligence had directed her to the hospital, and she could guess why. The Cyclan with its awesome power cast a wide shadow, working its will even when none of its servants were present. If another cyber had been present the room would have been sealed and guarded against any unauthorized entry. Had Avro's aides survived the accident at the falls the same. But they had died, as all Avro's companions had died, to leave him helpless and alone.

"They will be here soon," said Vaclav as if reading her thoughts. "A special ship is carrying Cyclan physicians to Lychen. They will take over. But, my lady, Avro must be alive when they do."

A threat implied with a hint. One backed by the reputation of the organization which spanned the known galaxy. Obey or pay for disobedience. Pay in the subtle destruction of the economy, the ruin of established Houses, the blasting of ambition and hope. If Avro died too soon Lychen would be ruined.

But Avro could tell her what she needed to know.

"He saw," she said. "He was there. He had to be. He knows how Angado died and who killed Perotto."

"He was helpless. Unaware."

"When you discovered him, yes, but earlier?" Mirza shook her head. "I doubt it. And why was he present at all? Or the woman? No. There are too many questions left unanswered. He will answer them.''

Vaclav caught her arm as she stepped toward the bed. He was sweating, fear overriding the inherent danger of the act. To her the contact of his hand was an insult, an offense against her pride.

''My lady! For God's sake! A touch could kill him!''

The truth and she recognized it and she halted to look down at the skull-like features. A fool, she thought dispassionately. A man who had become a living, thinking machine. One who regarded food as fuel for his body and fat as unwanted surplus. An attitude which robbed him of needed reserves so that in times of strain he drew on basic needs and when, as now, he needed the energy to aid healing, it was not available.

Yet a clever man despite the stupidity. One who could take a handful of facts and extrapolate from them to formulate the logical outcome of any sequence of events. The power of the Cyclan; to guide those who hired their services and to assure success. To become so indispensable that they and not those who used them became the real rulers of worlds, the real dictators of policy. The power behind the throne, unrecognized, unassailable, undefeatable—in time they would own everything.

But not yet and never her.

''Please, my lady!''

Vaclav's hand fell from her arm as again she stepped toward the bed, but she made no effort to touch the patient, looking, instead, at the roll of record paper spilling from a monitoring machine at his side. She frowned in puzzlement at the patterns, checking the machine before again studying the paper.

A push-button was set in an oblong of plastic close to Avro's limp hand. She thrust her thumb against it, held it down until a nurse came running into the room.

"What—" The girl stared, eyes wide with shock. "You! What are you doing here? This room—"

"I ordered Kooga to meet me here." Mirza cut short the protest. "Where is he?"

"Doctor Kooga is off-duty. Resting. He—"

"Get him up and get him here. Fast!" The snap in her voice made the nurse jump. "Move, damn you! Get him!"

"But you shouldn't be here. It isn't allowed. The regulations—" Flustered, the girl turned toward the door, relaxed as she saw the man filling the opening. "This is Doctor Kooga."

He was tall, slim, a face masked by the need to maintain detachment, one too used to the sight of pain. A man younger than Vaclav, who was a decade younger than herself. His voice, while calm, held the tone of one accustomed to obedience.

"Why are you here, nurse?"

"The bell summoned me, sir. When I arrived these people were present."

"Thank you. You may go." He waited until her footsteps had faded down the passage. "Now I suggest we have less shouting and less giving of orders. In themselves neither is capable of achievement." He looked at Vaclav. "I think I know you—Chief Guardian, correct?" He continued at Vaclav's nod. "We've been having a little trouble lately over unauthorized parking. Too many have grown into the habit of leaving their vehicles too close to the hospital. It causes congestion and noise we can do without. See to it."

Vaclav closed his lips against the bile rising from his stomach.

"And you, madam?"

"I am the Lady Mirza Annette Karroum. I have an interest in your patient. But first let me ask you about the patterns you are getting on your encephalograph. They are most unusual and—"

"A matter for medical confidence." Kooga was bland as he interrupted. "The patient is in good hands and is as comfortable as can be expected in the circumstances. Now that your curiosity has been satisfied you may leave. The Chief will escort you from the premises."

She said, "Chief Vaclav will leave us. You will remain." To Vaclav she said, "I'll see you later."

Dismissal which he accepted but in the passage he paused, looking at a reflective surface, not proud of what he saw. A man too old, too established in set ways; he had somehow lost his original zest. Not as tall as he would have liked, not as slim, and far less handsome. Not as clever as the doctor who held the literal power of life and death in his hands. He could only hold and question and send for trial or release. Suffer the burning of stomach acids eating into ulcers when he was forced to swallow his pride. Know tormented nights when, for expediency, he acted more like a servant than a free man. Feel self-revulsion when he was spoken to like a dog and treated like an object of contempt.

Maybe he should have let the bitch kill the cyber and so make an end.

In the room Kooga waited as before for the sound of departing footsteps to fade then he said, firmly, "Let us get one thing straight, madam. Here I am the master. I give the orders. I am the one to be obeyed."

"You are bold," she said. "But stupid. I rule the Karroum—does that mean nothing to you?"

"It means you're rich but—"

"I own this hospital. I own the research facilities attached to it. I probably own your house and the schools your children attend. You have children?"

"Two boys and a girl. What has that to do with it?"

"Children and a wife and, maybe, dependent relatives all enjoying the good things of life. All coming from you, Doctor, and, through you, from me. What promises have the Cyclan made?" She pursed her lips as he made no answer. "Wealth? Position? A place in one of their hospitals?"

"They will appreciate all I do for Cyber Avro."

"So it seems you have a choice. You can rely on their promises or risk the certainty of my anger. On the one hand you stand to gain—what? On the other you will lose your position here. You will lose your house. Your children will be denied their schools. No one claiming affinity with the Karroum will employ you. You will be ostracized. You, your wife, your children, your relatives—need I say more?"

He said, flatly, "You can't. You wouldn't."

"You challenge my power?" Her face became ugly. "I could break you as you could break that nurse who came in here. This is your world, Kooga, but it is only a part of mine. Who is going to fight for you? Who will dare to defy me? Within a year you'll be ruined, your children begging in the streets. And never think I'd hesitate at doing it. The honor of the Karroum is at stake. Make your choice, Doctor."

The promise of friendship from a vast power against the angry spite of a fanatical old woman. If he refused her would the Cyclan restore what she would take? And what if, despite his care, Avro should die before they arrived?

He said, "The pattern from the encephalograph is dictated by an unusual growth in the cyber's cortex. A mass of what seems to be alien tissue which has become incorporated with the basic structure."

"Alien? A cancer?"

"I'm not too sure. The Cyclan has ordered no samples to be taken or investigations made. Those advising me seemed to be aware of the condition and ordered me to take steps to relieve the pressure. This I did by extensive trepanning. The exposed areas of the brain are now covered with plastic domes containing a sterile vapor.''

The brain almost naked, pulsing beneath transparent bowls, the whole covered with dressing to hold them in place and hide them from view. And she had been tempted to slap the lax and empty face!

''Can he be revived enough to talk?'' She altered the question. ''Does he have periods of loquacity?''

''At times he rambles but seems to be unaware of what is near. Almost it is as if he is vocalizing dreams.''

''Such as?''

''Birds. Flying. Falling.'' Kooga shrugged. ''Just ramblings.''

''Does he answer direct questions?'' Again she altered the question. ''Can you arrange for him to do so?''

''He is resting in a delicate metabolic balance and to stimulate his consciousness could have unfortunate results. His constitution is poor and I am attempting to bolster it. He is too weak for slow time to be effective—he would die of starvation before any cure could be effected. The alternative, cryogenic treatment, I am reserving for any later emergency.''

Frozen, drugged, held in suspended animation with all life-processes slowed. Had Kooga already used it Avro would be beyond her reach. Thoughtfully Mirza looked at him, at the push-button by his limp hand.

"Why the bell if you don't expect him to revive?"

"An elementary precaution. Aside from the growth in his skull he isn't really ill. His distress is caused by side effects of the pressure and, if it could be removed, he might regain full use of his faculties. In such cases remissions are common. Momentary flashes of awareness or periods which could last some time."

"In which he would be lucid?"

"Of course. There is no viral or bacteriological infection. No broken bones. No organic degeneration to flood the system with toxic wastes. His sense of awareness is distorted by the growth which has disorganized his normal cerebral function."

Like a tumor causing headache, madness and final death. Pain through inpact with the appropriate center, apathy, loss of muscular control. And yet Kooga claimed he wasn't really ill. Not in the strict medical sense, maybe, but certainly in the engineering. Yet, if he had remissions, he could still be of help.

She told Kooga how and he frowned.

"It will be difficult."

"Tell me how? All we need is a bone-conductor speaker and a larynx-mike. I'll make a tape for continuous play. If it breaks into his awareness he'll know what I want. If he has a remission he'll be able to whisper the answer." She added, sensing his waning reluctance, "Do it and you'll have my favor. Anything you get from the Cyclan will be a bonus."

"I won't risk his life."

"All I want is to use his ability. His special skill. The answer to a single question." She drew in her breath. "Where the hell to find Dumarest."

Chapter Four

He slept late, waking to find the window filled
with glowing light, uneasy at his tardiness. As he
stirred a pounding came from the door, sound
which must have woken him, and Dumarest reared
on the bed, calling out as his feet touched the
floor.

"What is it?"

"Please, sir, a message from my master. He
will receive you at zenith."

Baglioni's voice and Dumarest frowned. "When?
At noon?"

"At zenith, sir. Food is waiting your pleasure
downstairs."

Dumarest stood upright and felt a momentary
nausea. The product of too great an effort maintained too long or the lingering traces of an insidi-

ous drug. It could easily have been administered in the food or wine served at the dinner but if so for what purpose? He glanced at the door to his room, firmly held by a chair rammed beneath the knob, if he had been drugged to sleep deeply then no one had been able to get to him. Unless the intent had been merely to keep him out of the way.

Standing beneath the shower he recalled the final events of the previous night. Toyanna, Shior whom he had met later, a man built like a whip, slim, graceful, one who could have been a high-wire artist. Vosper who had played with a deck of cards and betrayed a gambler's skill. Others, faces and voices, among them Govinda's, and then the midget guiding him to his room.

To the bed in which he had slept like a log.

Ice-cold water lashed his body to drive away the last of his somnolence. The clothing he had worn at dinner lay where he had thrown it. He ignored it, donning his own, checking the edge of his knife before thrusting it into his boot. Downstairs a servant led him to a small chamber furnished with a table and chairs.

Lopakhin sat in one if them, eating, grease shining on his lips. He waved a fork in greeting.

"Earl! Good to see I'm not the only laggard. Help yourself." The fork pointed as he spoke, halting at the dishes on the table, many of them steaming. "Broiled fish in that one. Eggs in that. Spiced meat over there. Fruit, bread, porridge—God know's who eats it, and this holds something like jam. In the other pots is coffee or tisane. Two kinds, mint and something else." He busied himself with his food. "Don't stand on ceremony, just dig in."

Dumarest chose a portion of fruit, some of the porridge, a piece of bread accompanied by a cup of mint tisane.

Sitting he said, "Is every night like last night?"

"No. That was a special occasion."

"To greet me?" Dumarest added, "I was expected, but how did anyone know I was coming?"

"A call, maybe." Lopakhin wiped his mouth and put down his fork. "Someone you asked direction from could have warned Chenault you were coming." He saw the shake of Dumarest's head. "No?"

"I'd heard of Chenault but didn't know just how to find him. It took time to find out."

"And you didn't want to ask direct. Why? Because you didn't want anyone to know your destination. And you walked the last, what? Hundred miles?" Lopakhin pursed his lips in a soundless whistle. "I see what you're getting at."

"Things like that worry me," said Dumarest. ";I'd like to know how it was done."

Lopakhin looked at his plate as if trying to read an answer in the smeared mess of his food. Then, with an abrupt gesture, he pushed it aside.

"You've met Hilary. We fight and argue at times but we're close. Two of a kind but on her it shows more than it does on me. Can you imagine what it must have been like for her? A child, tormented, made different from any other she knew, set up as a spectacle to be laughed at, goggled at, used, abused. Most in that position would have become little better than animals. Some would have gone mad. A few could have found escape in some other way. Closing in on themselves and finding something inside of them they didn't know they had. A trait. A talent. Something given as compensation, maybe.''

"Like your artistry?"

"I didn't say that."

"I know. You were talking about Hilary." Dumarest pushed aside his barely touched food. "So she's a sensitive. Able to tell if strangers are approaching. Is that it?"

"Something like that."

"Is that why Chenault keeps her?" Dumarest rose as Lopakhin made no answer. "Never mind. It isn't important. But thank you for telling me."

"If you're one of us you should know. If not then it doesn't—" The artist broke off. "I'd rather you didn't mention who told you."

About the sensitive or the near-spoken threat? Dumarest thought about them both as he headed toward the great doors. They were locked but a postern yielded beneath his hand and he stepped into the clearing before the house. It was deserted, silent but for the musical tinkle of water, and he stepped across it to where the side of the valley reared high before him. A glance at the towering mountain still hiding the sun and he began to climb. Halfway up he halted to sit and look at the Valley of Light.

It was well named: at sunset it would be filled with golden hues, at night the burning darts of firebirds and the flare of other nocturnal creatures together with the sheen of plants releasing stored energy in pale effulgence. At dawn would be the ghosts of dying brilliance, the fading gleam of vanishing stars but now, with the sun sending streamers of brilliance to halo the mountain, it held a muted softness. A lambent glow in which details were blurred and perspective distorted.

A small world which Chenault had made his own. A house which was more like a castle. Guests and servants who acted as retainers. If they didn't accept him as one of their number would he be killed?

Lopakhin had hinted as much and it was a real warning. Had he been drugged to keep him somnolent while his fate had been decided? Did Chenault summon him as a friend or as an executioner?

"Earl!" He heard the voice and rose as Govinda called again. "Earl! Where are you!"

"Here!" He waved as he saw the scarlet flash of her hair. "I'm up here!"

"It's getting late." The pale blur of her face stared at him, framed by the mass of her hair, a face which, suddenly, became achingly familiar. "Earl?"

He stumbled as he ran toward her, his boot hitting a root, causing him to fall, to roll down the slope and come to rest hard against the gnarled bole of a stunted tree. One which showered him with droplets and eye-stinging pollen from the profusion of pendant tails adorning the branches. Rising, rubbing at his eyes, he saw her running toward him but now she looked as she had before.

"We must hurry." She looked at the sun now burning at the peak of the mountain. "It's zenith and Chenault will be waiting."

He sat in a room flanked with shelves bearing old books, moldering files, logs, reports, journals, ancient manifests, recordings dusty and faded with time. An assembly interspersed with brighter, newer items; globes, star charts, almanacs, computer readouts all set in neat array. The room was windowless, light coming from glow-plates set in the roof, a soft illumination which dispelled all shadows.

"My hobby." Chenault's gesture embraced the room. "Or my obsession, some would say. It rather depends on your point of view. Tell me, Earl, what do you know of legends?"

"I know that others claim that in every legend lies a grain of truth."

"Others? What of yourself?"

"I wouldn't know." He saw Chenault smile and added, bluntly, "You know why I'm here and what I'm looking for but what I hope to find is no myth. Earth exists. I know it. I was born on that world. To me it is no legend."

"But to others it is nothing else."

Dumarest shrugged. "A point of view. Some would say you are mad for wasting your time with old papers and idle dreams. Because they say it does it make it true? A man I trusted told me you

58

could and would help me. That is why I'm here. If he was wrong tell me and I'll leave.''

"He wasn't wrong.''

"Shakira,'' mused Dumarest. "The circus of Chen Wei. He owned it but he hadn't founded it. That was done long ago. By your father? Your grandfather?''

Chenault said, "How did you know?''

"Your name. The appearance of your hall. Those you keep around you. Once the circus gets into your blood you can't get rid of it. Chen Wei— Chenault, the coincidence is too strong. Do you ever regret letting it go?''

"At times, yes. Then it is like a pain. But I had no choice and Tayu's need was greater than my own. We reached agreement and I retired to follow my own pursuits. The money from the sale allowed me to do that, to help others and . . . and . . . well, all that is history. But, yes, I did know you were coming and what you hoped to gain.'' Chenault smiled, relaxing. "You're a hard man, Earl. I knew it the moment I saw you. A hard and determined man. Only a fool would take you for one. Now, let us talk about legends.''

A subject which had become his life and he glowed as he spoke of mythical worlds, of strange regions reputedly discovered and later forgotten, of mystical plants and beasts, of isolated areas on lost and forgotten planets. Tales Dumarest had heard before but he sat patiently, listening, waiting, knowing the other must take his time.

"Eden, Paradise, Heaven, Avalon—all legendary worlds, Earl. All with one thing in common; places of ease and beauty where pain is unknown and no one ever falls sick or grows old or dies. Hope-worlds, Pearse calls them. Planets built of imaginative longing. Born in conditions of despair and hardship; tales whispered to children to console them for their bleak and hopeless lives. Live, be good, and when you die those worlds will be waiting. With time the essential qualification became forgotten and now men actually believe such worlds exist and are waiting to be rediscovered together with others, El Dorado, Jackpot, Bonanza —a dozen others including Earth."

"Which is no legend."

"Pearse says otherwise. Have you read him? And the study by Mikhailovik on the subject? The work of Dazym Negaso?" Chenault rose and moved to a shelf to return with a thick volume. "The third edition," he said, "Completely revised. Listen." He turned pages then, in a flat voice, read, "Earth, the name of a mythical planet held in veneration by the Original People, a backward sect found on various planets scattered throughout the galaxy. The sect is a secret one and neither seeks nor welcomes converts, fresh adherents being obtained from natural increase. The main tenet of their belief is that Mankind originated on a single world, the mythical planet Earth, and after cleansing by tribulation, Mankind will return to the supposed world of origin." Chenault closed the book. "Well?"

"There is more," said Dumarest. "He talks of the Original People and their esoteric rites. He also mentions the inconsistency of a variety of human types developing on one world beneath one sun."

"The main argument of those eager to discount the theory," said Chenault. "But all using it overlook the obvious. We have varied types of human now, yes, those with black skins and with brown, with yellow and white together with a range of hair colors and consistencies; curled, lank, oval, round, kinked—and even divergencies in physical shape; long-armed, broad-shouldered, round-headed and peaked. But all can interbreed. All belong to the same species. To any ethnologist the answer is obvious." Chenault set down the book and leaned forward over the table at which he sat. "One race, Earl. One type—the changes took place after leaving the Mother Planet. After!"

Born of wild radiations found in space and on worlds close to violent suns. Genes altered to form new patterns. Mutations many of which must have died as unviable but some had survived to pass on their altered characteristics. Dumarest had seen them; catlike men, wolflike, women who had the markings of serpents, haired like goats, some with skin thickened in places into scales. And Chenault must have seen more; things of nightmare, creatures distorted beyond easy recognition, shaped in mockeries of birds, beasts, spiders, fish.

Freaks to stock sideshows.

"It fits, Earl," he said. "If Mankind originated

on one world they couldn't be as they are now. The changes must have come after they had left. Perhaps they had to leave because of the changes." He paused. Then, in a voice which held the roll of drums, he intoned, "From terror they fled to find new places on which to expiate their sins. Only when cleansed will the race of Man be again united."

The creed of the Original People—was Chenault one of them? But if he was why had he revealed himself? Or was he throwing out bait to win support and, maybe, more information?

Dumarest said, "You are confusing legends. As I understand it Earth is supposed to be a world loaded with riches. Rivers of medicinal wine, trees heavy with fruit, hills studded with gems. Find it and you find the wealth of the galaxy."

"The things left behind," said Chenault. "The goods which had to be left, the installations, the buildings, the facilities, the treasure of knowledge, Earl. Of knowledge. Can you imagine what secrets they must have known? No, there is no conflict. Not when you study it with an open mind. Not when you delve a little beneath the surface. Did you know that Earth has another name?"

Dumarest nodded. "Terra."

"Exactly. Now it begins to make sense." Again Chenault intoned the creed. "From terror they fled . . . Not 'terror,' Earl, but Terra. Terra! They ran from Earth!"

*　　*　　*

It made sense but words, like figures, could be made to supply a variety of truths. Chenault had chosen his some time ago; despite the timbre of his voice, the deduction wasn't new, and Dumarest remembered the ritual of the blessing, the symbolic gesture and the words intoned, the response.

He said, "Tayu, Tama, Toetzer, Toyanna, Tyner—how many of you have names beginning with T?"

"Why?"

"It's a mistake unless you want to advertise yourselves. Coincidence can be stretched too far. And if you're using it as a means of identification there are better ways."

"Such as this?" Chenault made the gesture he had made at the table, hands forming a T. "How many would know what it means? Would you? But if I did this?" He drew a T on the table with a finger dipped in ink. At the upper junction he added a circle then, deliberately, quartered it with a cross.

"The symbol of Earth," said Dumarest. "Of Terra. But I'm not interested in legends. All I want is to get back home."

"We share the same ambition."

"You act like a secret society. Why? There is no need."

"No?" Chenault leaned across the table. "I don't agree. Think about it, Earl. How long have you searched for the coordinates of Earth? How often have you been frustrated? If the planet exists, and you know that it does, why can't it be found?''

A question Dumarest had pondered too often and still the answers remained the same. It wasn't listed in the almanac and, as all planets were listed, it couldn't exist. The logical answer which refused to recognize its absence of logic. Another, equally vapid: Earth was a legend and who could believe a legendary world was real? And how could an actual world have such a stupid name? Earth was dirt, soil, the stuff you grew crops in. Worlds had proper names or they weren't worlds at all.

Words to deny the obvious, but men believed in them and not his living, breathing assertion of the truth. To state it was to invite mockery, contempt, arrant disbelief. A weaker man would have been made the butt of cruel jests, one less controlled would have wasted strength in angry combat.

"A lost world," mused Chenault. "Your world, I mean. You left it, wandered on the ship which carried you and, when you tried to return home you found no one believed it to be real. Well, stranger things have happened. I remember one time when—" He broke off, one hand lifting to his chest.

"Something wrong?"

"No. Give me a moment." Chenault lowered his head as if to hide his face and eyes. Time during which Dumarest sat listening, his face impassive, his eyes half-closed. "Forgive me."

Chenault straightened in his chair. "The penalty of age."

"You want me to get something? Water? Wine? Some brandy?"

"No."

"A doctor?"

"No. I'll be—" Again the hand lifted as Chenault almost slumped to the table. Dumarest rose, touched his shoulder, the exposed column of the throat. "No!" Chenault twisted. "Leave me. Get—" His voice faded. "Tell her I need her. Hurry!"

"Who?"

"Pia. Pia. Tell her."

Dumarest left the room, almost running, reaching the dining room, a chamber holding musical instruments, another set with gaming tables. Vosper sat dealing himself a hand.

"Chenault's ill. He wants the woman, Toyanna. Where can I find her?"

"The laboratory or in her room on the first floor but—" He shrugged as Dumarest moved away, concentrating on his cards.

Pia Toyanna was halfway down the stairs when Dumarest found her. She wore a simple gown, green edged with black, belted snug to her slender waist. She carried no satchel and her hands were empty. She listened to Dumarest with an air of impatience.

"Yes. Yes, I understand." She nodded dismissal. "Just leave this to me."

"Do you need help?" Chenault was a big man. "If he needs to be moved you could have trouble."

"I can manage." She faced him, eyes and voice determined. "You've done all you can do. Now please leave things to me."

Dumarest watched her go, following her as she headed to where he had left Chenault, frowning when she moved on to a door lower down the passage. As he made to follow a figure stepped before him. Baglioni, small but determined, lifted his left hand. The dart gun in the other glimmered with reflected light.

"This area is restricted, sir. Please do not force me to use this against you." The dart gun lifted in his hand.

Dumarest said, "Do you think it would stop me?"

"I'm certain of it." The midget remained calm. "It fires a spray with a cover four feet in diameter at a distance of as many yards. I shall fire as soon as you lessen that distance. One dart must surely hit your face and one will be enough to knock you out. To cost you an eye, perhaps, if you should be unlucky. Personally I wouldn't care to gamble on the odds."

Too high against him but not for Dumarest. He knew he could close the distance between them and reach the man before he could fire. But to do it would reveal his speed and make an enemy and all to no purpose. Chenault had the right to act as he chose within his own house.

Casually Dumarest said, "I wouldn't either. Will Tama be all right?"

"He will receive the best of attention, sir. That I assure you. You need have no concern. Now, if you would care to return to the dining room, refreshments have been served."

Cakes and sandwiches and drinks of various types together with a collection of condiments.

Vosper, selecting a cake, sprinkled it with an aromatic red powder and tasted it with the tip of his tongue.

"Too sweet." He added more powder. "You shouldn't have been in such a hurry, Earl. I could have saved you that run-in with Baglioni. And Toyanna knew she was needed."

"Why didn't she go directly to Chenault?"

"Didn't she?" Vosper shrugged. "Maybe she went to get her medical kit. She couldn't have done much for Tama without one." He tasted the cake again, nodded his satisfaction, and began to eat. "Care for a game? Anything you like as long as it's for real money. I lose interest when playing for fun. Your choice; Starsmash, Spectrum, High, Low, man-in-between. You name it."

"Poker?"

"Sure." Vosper beamed. "My favorite." Finishing his cake he glanced toward the gaming room. "Want to eat or shall we get at it?"

"You sound like a shark," said Dumarest. "Are you?"

"No."

"A telepath? How did you know about my run-in with the midget?"

"A shrewd guess. When Tama's in trouble Baglioni comes running to protect him. It happens every time." Vosper laughed. "A telepath. I wish to hell I was. I'm just an engineer."

Chapter Five

Like a mouse the nurse moved down the corridor and into the room where Avro lay like a corpse on the bed. A routine visit; monitors did a good job and normally were trusted but this was a special patient and Doctor Kooga had made it plain that any failure would bring harsh penalties.

Quietly she stepped to the side of the bed, looking at the flaccid, skull-like face, one seeming more dead than alive, yet the monitors registered the beating of the heart, the passage of oxygenated blood through the brain. Only one thing seemed out of place: a tiny, flickering lamp on the panel of the encephalograph, the signal of high current demand. Nothing to worry about, activity of the recording pens always registered above a certain level, but this was unusual in terms of duration.

The cyber's mental faculties were working at high pressure and she wondered why. He should be comatose, drifting in a mindless lethargy, thoughts at a low ebb. Instead his mind seemed to be acting like a dynamo.

Leaning over the inert form she gently touched his face. A gesture without the intention of a caress; part of her duties was to administer drops in each eye. A thing done with practiced skill and she wiped the surplus from the waxen cheeks, trying not to think of the orbs she had seen, the spark which seemed to glow in their depths. The reflection of light, she guessed, it had to be that. The cyber was drugged, asleep, resting like the dead man he would soon be unless things took a turn for the better.

Even so she tiptoed quietly from the room when she left.

Avro didn't register her going. He floated in a void shot through with swaths of warmly glowing colors illuminating shapes of unusual proportions. Vistas which rolled endlessly through the chambers of his mind. Stored impressions, memories, speculations, all now released to flood his questing awareness, but confined to the limits of his brain.

A foretaste of what would be when his cortex had been removed from his body and sealed in a vat to become a part of the tremendous complex which was Central Intelligence. There he would become one with the gestalt which directed the Cyclan, using cybers and agents to spread the dominance of the organization until, in the end, it would rule the entire galaxy.

A concept which yielded mental pleasure and he swam in a sea of ceaseless attainment during which problems were solved, new worlds based on unusual chemical combinations created, new frames of reference established to bring into being new and exciting universes.

A time of euphoria which faded as the colors dulled and the vast shapes diminished to form a rocky plain on which stood a solitary figure. One clad in the scarlet robe he knew so well, the breast glimmering with the Seal of the Cyclan.

Marle? Had the Cyber Prime come to visit him in his vision? A companion? Someone he had previously known? Avro strained his eyes but could make out no detail; the drawn cowl masked the figure's face.

"Master?"

His words died without acknowledgment but he was not surprised. The vision matched others he had experienced before; illusions born of his distorted mind. The Homochon elements grafted within his brain were now growing like a cancer running wild. Normally, when activated, they established rapport with Central Intelligence, placing him in direct mental communication with the great complex. An organic communication which was almost instantaneous. But, illusion though it seemed, this too could be the product of rapport.

He said, "Who are you? Am I to be interrogated?"

Sound which did not exist beyond his enclosed

world, just as the movement he made as he stepped toward the figure had no reality but in his mind.

"You failed," said the cowled figure. "You failed."

Not once but twice and Avro felt the shame of inadequacy even as he admitted the truth.

"I admit it," he said. "I failed. But it was not wholly my fault. The affliction I now suffer struck me down. I had Dumarest in my hand, safe, captured, but I collapsed at the wrong moment. Even so he should have been held. The arrangements had been made. Those with me should have taken him." In memory he was again the sight over the falls; the rafts almost touching, the flames, the bodies falling and Dumarest rising like a bird into the sky. "Luck," he said. "I knew of his luck but thought I'd taken every precaution. I made a mistake, one, but it was enough. Who could have known I would be stricken down when I was?"

"You had the data. You knew of your condition."

"Yes."

"You should have predicted the logical outcome."

"I did. But there was time."

"Time is a variable."

"A trait accounted for. The probability of my staying active and successfully completing the capture was 98.5 percent. Almost certainty."

But it nor any other prediction could ever be that. Always there remained the unknown factor which, as had happened, could negate the highest probability. A factor which seemed to act to Dumarest's advantage with consistent regularity.

"Even so you failed. A proof of your inefficiency. Can you deny that you merit the penalty of failure?"

Avro felt the cold chill of what was to come. A cyber did not fail. If he did not succeed then he ceased to be a cyber. The reward for which he had dedicated his life was denied him. Instead he was given total extinction.

And the colors would be gone, the shapes, the endless drifting in a void thronged with mental attainment. There would be no created worlds, no new universes, no communion with others of his kind. No near-immortality in which to plan domination and guide the Cyclan to the fulfillment of the master plan.

"No," he said. "I have not failed. Not yet."

"Then where is Dumarest? The secret of the affinity twin which he holds still eludes us. We must recover the sequence in which the fifteen biomolecular units must be assembled."

Avro said, "To repeat the obvious demonstrates a lack of efficiency. I am aware of the need to obtain the secret."

One which would give the Cyclan total domination over all others. By its use one intelligence could take over the body of another. Become that other, using the host as it willed, defying all barriers of time and space. Each cyber could control a ruler and the brains making up Central Intelligence could experience bodily life again and rid the

Cyclan of the fear that they hovered on the brink of insanity.

"He must be found," said the figure. "Where is he? What happened in the main salon of the apartment by the falls. What happened?"

"Dumarest killed and escaped," said Avro. "Killed the man who had killed." He couldn't think of names but the incident was clear.

"Where is Dumarest?"

"Gone." Rising into the featureless sky on a trail of flame. "Gone."

"Where is Dumarest?"

A problem to be answered; find the man and find the secret and, at the same time, prove his efficiency, his right to his reward. Avro examined the evidence, the smattering of facts he had gleaned as to what Dumarest had done since his arrival on Lychen. The people he had met and the interests he had shown. Data which he incorporated into a web of other facts, isolating, evaluating, arriving at a logical conclusion.

"Where is Dumarest?"

A question answered then ignored despite repeated demands as he concentrated on the figure standing on the rocky plain before him. A simulacrum created by Central Intelligence? A novel means of rapport? Something special to himself or was the whole thing a fantasy?

"Who are you?" he demanded. "Show me your face."

He watched as a hand rose to throw back the cowl. He felt no surprise; logic had told him who and what the figure must be and he stood, in the world of his mind, looking at the accuser who was himself.

Vosper said, "Open for five. Jem?"

Toetzer took his time, pursing his lips as he studied his cards, the middle finger of his left hand flicking the pasteboards. A habit Dumarest had noticed since the man had joined the game hours ago. As he had noticed others from those who had joined the school.

"Call and raise ten."

Toetzer wasn't bluffing. He played with mathematical skill; paying strict attention to the odds, assessing the worth of each hand, the potential of each draw. Massak was different, using guile to mask his real intent.

"I'll just lift that another five."

A killer waiting to strike. To use the power of his money to crush the opposition as he would use the strength of his body to destroy an enemy. Shior matched him but in a more subtle fashion. A rapier as compared to a club smiling as he, too, lifted the raise by an equal amount. A ploy to test the opposition, buying the right to act in his own manner, one akin to Massak's but not so blatantly obvious. A man who would appear to be a reckless fool—and who would take those who thought so for all they had when the time was ripe.

"Earl?" Vosper looked to where he sat. "You in?"

Dumarest shook his head, following the instinct

which told him to fold his hand. Lopakhin joined
him, grunting when Vosper met the raise and doubled it.

"Here it comes. The hammer. The trouble with
Ron is he's greedy."

But too engrossed in his own hand to pay due
attention to the others. Dumarest sat back in his
chair, looking, listening. The players had gathered
as Vosper had said they might and, as was the
habit of men playing cards, they talked. Small
talk, banter, jests, idle remarks but, from such talk
information could be gained. Dumarest had made
the most of the opportunity.

Vosper was an engineer, Toetzer a mathematician,
Massak a mercenary, Shior a fighter, Lopakhin,
aside from an artist, was also a communications
expert. Grain garnered from chaff and Dumarest
added it to other facts. Toyanna a skilled doctor,
Hilary a sensitive, Govinda?

He felt the touch on his shoulder as Massak,
laughing, scooped up his winnings. The woman
stood beside him, hair a scarlet aureole, her face
smooth, her eyes luminous.

Vosper glanced at her and shook his head.
Toetzer, cards in hand, paused as he was about to
deal.

"No offense, Earl, but if Govinda stays then
I'm quitting the game."

"You think she's helping me to cheat?"

"No, nothing like that, it's just that—" Toetzer
broke off, then appealed to the others. "How can I
explain? Can any of you tell him?"

"She reminds him of his mother," said Vosper. "The one who—"

"Not my mother!" Toetzer was harsh. "The bitch who bought me. Who defiled me. Who— The hell with it. She stays I go." He slammed down the cards. "What's it to be?"

"I'll go," said Govinda. Stooping, she whispered in Dumarest's ear. "I just wanted to be close to you. To ask if I'll see you again later. We could go for a walk or something."

"Yes," he said. "Later."

"Not now?"

He glanced at the cards, the players, the money on the table. As yet he still had to win. "Later," he said again. "I promise."

Massak shook his head as she left the room. "A beautiful woman," he said. "What do you see in her, Earl?" He hurried on as Dumarest frowned. "I mean what does she look like to you?"

"What you said—a beautiful woman."

"Yet she reminds Toetzer of everything he hates. To Vosper?" Massak looked toward him. "What do you see in her, Ron?"

"I had a sister once. She looks the same."

"Someone you loved and would never hurt, right?" Massak turned to Lopakhin. "And you? What do you see with your artist's eye?"

"Beauty." Lopakhin was curt. To Dumarest he said, "They're having a game with you. Toetzer doesn't like her, that's true, or he says he doesn't like her, which isn't the same thing. Personally I think he fell in love with the woman who bought him and taught him how to live. Certainly he can't forget her. If she stood naked and defenseless before him all he'd do would be to try and kill her with kisses.''

Toetzer said, "That's a lie!"

"When you look at Govinda you see her. Right?"

"Yes, but—"

"That proves it." Lopakhin shrugged and again looked at Dumarest. "She's a mentamorph," he explained. "It's a survival trait, I guess. She appears to those who might possibly threaten her as something they would never hurt. With Vosper it's his sister. With me it's a model I knew once and for whom I'd have walked over burning coals. Who Massak likes is anyone's guess but Shior had to stop him once when he tried to get his hands on the woman. And you, Earl? What does she look like to you?"

A woman, soft, appealing, one haunted by a hidden yearning.

One who, twice now, had wrung the strings of his heart.

The first he mentioned, the second he did not. Shior nodded, understanding, his voice serious as he said, "You've hit it, my friend. Govinda is more than what she seems. Inside of her she carries a deep hurt. Of all the gifts that anyone could offer her, motherhood is the one she would take."

"She's barren," said Vosper. "Sterile. God knows how much she spent and how hard she's tried but—" He shrugged. "The thing she wants most is the thing she can't have."

"Adoption?"

"The easy answer, Earl, and the most obvious solution, but it's not for her. She needs to have an affinity with the child. She isn't an ordinary woman and can't accept an ordinary baby. Toyanna could tell you why; it has something to do with the rejection syndrome, a mental repulsion due to her attribute." Vosper shook his head and sighed. "A pity. I hate to see anyone living in hell especially someone like Govinda. She's a nice person."

"Maybe too nice." Massak frowned at Toetzer. "Are you making love to those cards or stacking the deck? Come on, let's play."

Vaclav came out of the dusk like a nocturnal bird of prey, scowling, infuriated at the brusqueness of the command which had brought him to Kooga's office. To the doctor when they were together he snapped, "You summoned and I've responded. But if you have any more complaints as to unauthorized parking I shall not be amused."

"Sit." Kooga waved to a chair. Like the office it was of good quality and excellent taste. "Let us understand each other. As Chief Guardian of Lychen you have a duty to—"

"Protect the persons, property and privileges of the ruling Houses," interrupted Vaclav. "Basically that is the sum total of my responsibility. To take care of the Insham, the Vattari, the Cerney, the Karroum. Especially the Karroum."

"You don't like them?"

"They own most of the planet. They crack the

79

biggest whip. When they say 'jump' we ordinary people ask 'how high?' I think you know that, Doctor.''

"And if I do?''

"You have the answer to your question." Vaclav added, impatiently, "There are things needing my attention. Why did you send for me?"

"A problem." Kooga opened a drawer and produced a recording. He laid it before him on the desk. "After our last meeting Mirza Karroum had me do something for her. She was convinced the cyber could help her locate Dumarest. At her insistence I connected a microphone to an electrode connected to the cyber's cranium so as to feed in the output of a tape. I also connected another from his larynx to a recorder. It was her hope that, by verbal stimulus, he would gain remission and be able to respond."

Vaclav said, "Would it work?"

"Theoretically, yes."

"Did it?"

For answer Kooga touched the recording with the tip of a finger and said, "We are dealing with the Cyclan. On Lychen the Karroum are powerful but we both know that if the Cyclan wished they would be ruined and destroyed. Also, and this you can understand, I do not take kindly to threats."

Vaclav studied the doctor's face, seeing beneath the surface to the injured pride, the resentment which he knew so well. Familiar emotions which he had seen and used often before, but Kooga was not the subject for interrogation even if a charge could be made. Even so he could be led.

"So you made a decision," said Vaclav. "What?"

"This is in the strictest confidence, Chief."

"Of course."

"I had to make a decision and arranged a compromise. I made sure that the skull-connection was inoperative. The connecting wire wasn't quite making contact."

"So you got nothing." Vaclav mimicked a report. "Too bad, my lady, I did my best but the cyber failed to respond." He shrugged. "Where's the problem?"

"A nurse went into his room to make a routine check. During it she noticed unusual activity of the encephalograph. She also made physical contact with the patient. This was within the scope of her duties but—" Kooga paused then finished with a rush. "She must have moved the wire or touched the skull-connector and made it operable. She probably thought it a part of the monitoring device and did a routine check. This is the result." Again he touched the recording. "The final part contains the cyber's prediction of where Dumarest is to be found."

"Where?"

"Chenault's. The Valley of Light."

"Are you sure?"

"No. How can I be? The prediction comes from the cyber, not myself, but how often are they wrong?" Kooga frowned. "You seem troubled."

Vaclav said, "At Mirza Karroum's insistence I

ordered a wide-scan, high-fly survey. Costly, but
what the Karroum want they get. Something which
could have been the raft Dumarest used was spotted to the east of the mountain where Chenault has
his home. But it was over a hundred miles distant.
Why would he have wanted to walk so far?''

"To hide.''

"From us?''

"From the Cyclan. Listen.''

The voice from the recorder was weak, thin,
drifting from fast to slow as if time, for the speaker,
held a dimension different and more variable than
for others. Words which blurred, changed, struck
with sudden, crystalline clarity.

"It ends there,'' said Kooga. "The part where
he mentions Chenault. That's the part Mirza took
notice of.''

"She heard it?''

"I couldn't stop her. I thought the recording
would be blank so there was no need to antagonize
her. Later, after I'd played it again, I sent for
you.''

"Why?''

"I told you the encephalograph showed unusual
activity,'' said Kooga. "The wild variations from
the normal seemed to be aligned to these spoken
words. That was to be expected but there were
other, wilder variations, all unfamiliar, but it's my
guess there's a connecting link. The stimulus must
have jarred his awareness and concentrated it on a
special area. Now listen again. Really listen.''

Again the words, the thread of varying sound,

but this time Vaclav concentrated harder, using his skill and training to filter noise from the relevant data, to fill in the missing pieces.

As the recording ended Kooga said, "He was explaining what happened in the room. How Dumarest killed a man who had killed. That must have been Perotto. Then comes the interesting part; the reason the Cyclan are so interested in Dumarest. It seems he holds a secret they want. A pity it isn't made clear but there is no doubt as to his importance to them." Pausing he added, meaningfully, "His importance and his value."

"Alive."

"What?"

"Dead he would be valueless," explained Vaclav. "Mirza was right; he didn't kill Perotto in self-defense. If they fought it was because Perotto wanted to save his life. We know that he failed. Which makes Dumarest guilty of murder."

"A technicality." Kooga dismissed it with a gesture. "Avro was the only witness and he would never put the man he came to find in danger. Soon the representatives of the Cyclan will arrive on Lychen. If we can hand Dumarest over to them, alive and well, we can ask our own price. Do I make myself clear, Chief?

"You want me to find him, hold him, keep him from harm while you negotiate with the Cyclan."

"Yes." Kooga nodded, satisfied. "I assume you have no objections to making a fortune? To being rich and freed of your present restraints?"

"None."

"Then we are partners?"

Vaclav said, dryly, "In what? If Mirza Karroum knows where Dumarest is she's on her way to kill him by now."

Chapter Six

She came with the night, the stars, her rafts making dark, moving splotches against the nacreous glow of the sky. Riding high and proud as they arrowed toward the Valley of Light.

"Three of them." Massak lowered his binoculars. "She'll drop one to each side to provide crossfire and come in with the other." He sucked thoughtfully at his lower lip. "If we take her out the others will open up in revenge. If we hit them she'll blast the house. Clever. The lady must have had experience."

"That's good," said Shior from where he stood at the mercenary's side. "At least she'll know when she's been beaten."

"If she's beaten." Massak used his binoculars

again. "There's always doubt in these matters. Right, Earl?"

Dumarest made no comment, standing, watching the sky. The rafts were closer now, making no attempt to adopt evasive action, probably unaware they had been spotted. A reasonable assumption; Hilary's talents were unknown outside the house. Her warning had come in good time now that she, and others, were safely lodged in the cellars far below the surface.

Dumarest said, "How many and how are they armed?"

"Four in each of the side-rafts together with a driver. Five in all. Ten when put together. They seem to have machine rifles."

"Lights?"

"That too."

Men to spread along the facing crests, lights to illuminate the clearing, weapons to cover it with a murderous crossfire. Dumarest said, "We need to get behind them so as to attack from the rear. They'll be facing inward against the glow. Easy targets, but we'll have to be in position before they land."

"Good thinking, Earl." Massak smiled, teeth white against the ebon of his skin. "This isn't the first time you've seen action."

"No."

"I thought not. You have a way of sizing up the situation. How about the other raft? Any ideas?"

"Once the flankers are knocked out they'll be in the center of fire. We can hit them from both sides." Dumarest added, pointedly, "If we get into position in time."

"Us, Earl. Shior and me. This one you stay out of. Chenault's order." Massak glanced at the other man. "Let's go!"

As they vanished into the shadows Lopakhin called from the open postern.

"Earl! Here, man! Get inside—fast!"

Good advice and Dumarest followed it; if firing should start he would be a clear target. As the heavy door thudded shut behind him the artist gestured to a screen beside it.

"It's hooked to a scanner higher up," he explained. "A good view and a safe one. You never know what these crazy bastards will do next. Look at her!" He gestured at the screen, the raft it depicted, the woman standing within it. "What the hell does she imagine she is?"

A warrior-queen riding to war as others of her House had done in ages past. Snatching the power left by slain men to lead their forces to victory and establish the Karroum as the thing it was today. A Family secure in its pride, jealous of its honor.

As the raft lowered, her amplified voice echoed from the sides of the valley.

"Chenault! This is Mirza Annette Karroum! I demand audience!"

Silence then, as the raft landed, her voice again.

"Chenault! I come to parley. Unless you appear I'll blow open your house!"

A threat backed with the potential of action. As lights blazed from the flanking rafts to illuminate the clearing Dumarest could see the snouted weapon in the woman's vehicle. A heavy-duty laser or a missile-launcher. The latter, he guessed, a laser would have been less efficient given the vehicle and its load.

"Chenault, damn you! I'll wait no longer!"

"Wait!" His voice boomed from a speaker. "Give me time. Is this a way to come calling? What ails you that you make such threats? Has the Karroum gone mad?"

"This is a matter of honor. I shall not be denied."

"Honor? What is this talk of honor? How have I offended you? Why come with arms to my house? What do you want of me?"

"Open your doors. Come out and face me."

"Yes. Yes, but give me a moment. All can be settled with a little patience. Mirza Annette Karroum, you say?"

Talk to gain time as Dumarest knew and, on the crests, men would already have died if Massak and Shior knew their jobs. Gasping out their lives to the thrust of a blade or rearing, necks broken by the twist of a thong. Silent death dealt to the unsuspecting. A natural attribute of war.

Watching, Dumarest saw the woman look at her driver, speak to him, turn frowning to stare at the crests on either side. A loss of communication or some noise lacking explanation: something which troubled her.

He said, "If Chenault means to show he'd better do it fast. She's suspicious."

"He'll make it."

"Open the postern. Pretend he has. Hurry!"

He appeared as Lopakhin swung wide the panel, standing in the opening, gesturing as if to someone beyond. Mimicry made truth as Chenault stepped toward him. Past him. Through the door and out into the clearing to stand, tall and grim in the artificial glow.

A man who scant hours ago had collapsed now apparently in the best of health. His voice matched his stance, harsh, arrogant.

"This is my home. You intrude. Go before I feel insulted."

"Feel as you please. I stay until honor has been satisfied. Where is Dumarest?"

"Who?"

"Dumarest. Earl Dumarest. He is here and I want him. I want him dead. The honor of the Karroum demands it." She leaned forward over the snouted weapon in the raft, her face made ugly by light and shadow, flesh and blood turned into a chiaroscuro of ice and iron forming the lineaments of a bestial mask. "Him or you, Chenault. Make your choice. Your life, your home, all you possess— or you give me Dumarest. And you give him to me now!"

There was power in her and determination and an iron will which would brook no interference, no opposition. She would gain her way or do as she had threatened and, even as Chenault made no move, Dumarest knew that time was running out.

"Earl!" Lopakhin tried to catch his arm as

Dumarest reached for the door. 'Don't, man. Don't! Let Chenault handle it!''

A man who stood as if turned to stone, his head uptilted a little, his arms held from his body, shoulders stooped and strangely at variance with the massive torso.

As Dumarest came level with him Chenault turned and said, tightly, ''Go back. Don't interfere. Just leave things to me.''

''I can't.''

''Why not?''

Because if the man was killed the hope of finding Earth would go with him. The knowledge stored in his brain, the facts he must have garnered, the coordinates Dumarest felt he must have. And if he defied the woman he would die. The weapon mounted on the raft would fire and spread a hail of destruction. Shrapnel and flame which would turn the clearing and all it contained into smoldering ash.

The woman would do it. Even if she died giving the order yet she would still give it.

Dumarest walked toward her to halt in the pool of illumination thrown by the light on her raft.

He said, ''You want me. Why?''

''You are Dumarest?''

''Yes.''

''I came to kill you. I want you to know that.''

''I know it.'' He met her eyes. ''Now tell me why.''

''Why I want you dead?'' She stepped from the

raft and came close to him, her eyes raking his face, his body. "You killed one of the Karroum. That is answer enough."

"For you, obviously. But not for me. I assume you are talking of Perotto. I killed him, yes. If I hadn't he would have killed me. As he had already killed Angado. Or didn't you know that? Angado was of the Karroum, too. In fact he was the titular head of the House. Would you have hunted down Perotto if he were still alive? Or does the honor of the Karroum stop when it comes to dealing with murdering filth bearing the same name?"

"You go too far!" She fought for breath, trying to master her rage, mouth open as she filled her lungs. "Perotto was—"

"A killer. One without the guts to face his victim face to face. An assassin in the dark. One who paid others to do his dirty work." Dumarest fired the words like bullets. "Scum, as you'd admit if you weren't so blind in your prejudice. I killed him to save my life."

"No!" She was vehement in her denial. "He would never have killed you!"

The truth, but how did she know it? Only at the last when, knowing he would die, had Perotto tried to eliminate his destroyer. Working for the Cyclan he knew the value they placed on their quarry. Knew too how ruthless would be his punishment if he had failed to obey their orders. Avro? Had the cyber managed to survive? Had he told the woman what had happened?

A possibility and Dumarest considered it. One which could lead to an even greater danger than the one he was in. Armed, with Chenault as a hostage, who could stop the woman from taking him prisoner?

"My lady, let us understand each other." He faced her, smiling, at his ease. A man talking to an equal on a subject they could both appreciate. "I killed Perotto and I admit it. But it was a matter of honor as I'm sure you will agree. In fact I had no choice." He made a small gesture with his hands. "As you feel that you have no choice. Honor is a hard master to those who follow its dictates."

She said, tightly, "Explain."

"Perotto killed Angado. He was my friend. In fact I owed him my life. What else could I have done?"

The question was like a slap in the face and she stood, considering it, sensing that, somehow, she was being manipulated. A feeling which stiffened her earlier resolve.

"Nothing, perhaps, but for each action there is a penalty. Your honor has been satisfied. That of the Karroum has not. As you had to kill so must you be killed. Mharl!" A figure loomed behind her, a weapon lifted in its arms. "Aim and—"

"No!" The voice echoed from the crest as Massak shouted. "Fire and you're dead!" The bark of a rifle tore the air, slugs ripping into the ground, whining from buried stone. "Lower that gun. Lower it, I say!"

"My lady?"

"Obey." She didn't turn to look at the man. To Chenault she said, "What does this accomplish? Tonight you win—tomorrow your house will lie in rubble. How can you hope to oppose me?"

"I must try."

That answer gained nothing; trying he would fail and, failing, all would be lost. Dumarest glanced at him, then back to the woman, remembering how she had appeared on the screen, standing upright in the raft, face and body belonging to another age. As her code of honor belonged to a time long past. One of chivalrous concepts which had probably never existed but which still lingered to exert their charm.

He said, "There is a way, my lady . . . to settle this dispute with honor. To end it here and now and for all time. The old way." He saw by her eyes she understood. "The way of those who tread the narrow path. One against the other and let right prevail."

Trial by combat—he'd had no other choice.

Mharl was her champion, tall, younger than Dumarest by a decade, strong from a lifetime of arduous labor. Stripped, his torso was ribbed and roped with muscle, his biceps huge, the pectorals betraying his bull-like strength. A machine of flesh and brawn equipped with a shrewd and agile mind.

93

He stood poised, like a dancer, his eyes darting flickers beneath his brows.

In turn Dumarest studied the opposition.

Like Mharl he was stripped down to pants and boots; garments which gave mutual protection and offensive capability. A kick, correctly placed, could kill as effectively as a club or gun or knife. Weapons banned because of the advantage they could give to one or the other. In matters of honor Mirza liked to be precise. But her champion was trained, accustomed to wrestling, kicking, fighting with his hands. This Dumarest sensed from the way he stood, moved, shifted to present himself, the hands crossed before his loins, his weight always resting on one foot so as to free the other to kick.

"Ready?" Mirza Karroum looked from one to the other. "You know the rules: the first to yield admits defeat." An arrangement not as fair as it seemed; if Dumarest yielded he would admit his dishonor and merit summary execution. A fact she chose to ignore. "Begin!"

Dumarest moved, circling to put his back against the light, facing Mharl with the watching windows of the house before him. A small advantage, but lost as the man moved in turn, then, before he could settle, Dumarest dived in, throwing himself down to pivot on one hand, his boot lashing out to slam against Mharl's left knee.

That blow should have crippled but did no more than bruise; Mharl jumping back as it landed. A move preparatory to his own attack and he came in before Dumarest could regain his feet, kicking out, the toe of his boot like a club as it slammed against the hip. As Dumarest grabbed at it Mharl closed in, the hammer of his fists beating at Dumarest's face and torso, leaving ugly welts on the body, the taste of blood in the mouth.

The tattoo ended as Dumarest backed away, stooped, appearing more badly hurt than he was.

"Soon, my lady!" Mharl, excited, called the promise. "Soon honor will be satisfied."

The talk gained Dumarest time. He came in, watchful, noting the position of the hands, the feet, the tilt of the head. Ready when Mharl struck to dodge the blow, to strike in turn, to parry a driving fist, to strike at the corded throat, the edge of his stiffened hand lashing at the windpipe.

Speed offset by the other's massive build, his trained reactions.

Skill gained in the gymnasiums, added to by harsh experience, but Dumarest had lived longer, harder, had learned more. Stooping, he grabbed dirt, flung it into the other's eyes, followed it with a low attack, fist driving into the junction of the thighs. As Mharl screamed he struck again, higher, lifting a boot to rasp its edge down the man's shin. Stabbing at the eyes with his hand formed into a blunted spear, using the other to again attack the throat as Mharl threw back his head to defend his sight.

And felt the universe explode as hands crashed against the sides of his head.

Blows which would have killed had they been delivered with a little more force, a little more direction. Twin hammers driving at his ears in near-synchronization as Mharl, desperate, gambled on a quick victory. One he lost as Dumarest backed, blood streaming from his nose to dapple his chin, his naked torso.

"Mharl!" Mirza Karroum snapped her instructions. "Be wary. Wear him down. Don't let him get too close."

Good advice but Dumarest didn't let him follow it. Again he closed in, kicking, slashing, parrying the driving punches of the other man. Using his arms as if they had been swords, his hands as if they had been knives. Calling on the hard-won experience which had saved him so often before.

A blur and flesh yielded to his attack, blood marring the other's mouth and torso to match his own. Another and Dumarest grunted as a fist ground into his stomach, his own hand reaching out, stabbing, the tips of his fingers hitting the throat and driving deep. A blow followed by another in the same place then, as Mharl doubled, retching for breath, Dumarest was on him from behind, one arm rising to lock beneath the chin, the other completing the vise which held the head hard against his shoulder.

"Yield!" Dumarest jerked at his arm. "Yield, you fool, before I break your neck!"

He sensed rather than felt the lifted foot, the savage, backward kick which would have shattered bone had it landed. As Mharl staggered, his balance lost, Dumarest freed his right hand, lifted it, slammed it down hard on the other's temple.

As it locked back into place he said, "Why die when there's no need? Yield and let's have done with it."

"No! I—"

The words died as Dumarest crushed his left forearm against the windpipe. Against him Mharl squirmed, blood smearing, making a sticky film. As, again, he tried to kick, Dumarest sprang upward and wrapped his legs around the other's waist.

"Your last chance, Mharl. Yield or die."

It was no empty threat. Dumarest felt strength drain from him as he fought to retain his hold. Mharl was too dangerous to be given a chance, too determined to be underestimated. Too strong to be resisted if he should break free.

"Don't be a fool, man! Lift up your hands. Yield!"

A long moment then, as the hands fought to grip him, Dumarest began to close the vise formed by his arms. One powered by the muscles of his back and shoulders, the biceps, the corded sinews of his arms.

Mharl sagged, hands lifting to tear at the constriction, twisting, dropping to his knees as the pressure increased. He was dying, ears filled with the roar of his own blood, vision darkening, his chest a flame from need of air. Yet he would never yield: if nothing else he had pride.

A fact Dumarest guessed and, as Mharl fell toward the dirt he released his hold, lifted a hand, struck once and stood up with the unconscious man at his feet.

"My lady? Do you accept defeat?"

"He did not yield! He—"

"Is beaten." Chenault spoke from where he had stood, watching. "Would you prefer him dead? Dumarest was kind but if he made a mistake it can be rectified. Earl, if her honor demands it, finish the job. Kill him."

He said nothing, watching her face, the play of emotions it portrayed. In the old days things had been more simple; a champion won or he died and those for whom he fought did not have to make life or death decisions. Or so, at least, the stories she had heard as a child had convinced her. As they had instilled the concept of honor which had led to Mharl lying on the dirt at her feet.

Dumarest said, "He did his best for you. He fought well and tried to kill me. Despite that I'm willing to spare him. Are you?"

For a moment she hesitated, then, with an abrupt gesture, extended her hands before her, palms uppermost.

"Honor is satisfied. Right has prevailed. The dispute between us is ended. I offer you my friendship."

He accepted by placing his hands on her own. Beneath his fingers her skin was dry, rougher than he would have expected, warm with a febrile heat.

A woman tricked by her femininity, responding to his maleness, the euphoria of witnessed combat. Catching his fingers, holding them as, on the ground at their feet, Mharl groaned and twisted in his waking pain.

Chapter Seven

Lifting his goblet Massak said, "A thing neatly done, Earl. If ever you are in need of employment I know a dozen who would give you rank and a command. I salute you!"

He drank and Lopakhin followed his example. "Fast," he said as he lowered his glass. "The way you moved in, dodged, reacted—like lightning. Mharl didn't stand a chance."

A lie as he must have known; no fight could ever be a certainty and Mirza's champion had been dangerous with speed and skills of his own. Dumarest turned from the group around the table set in the great hall. Vosper's doing or Baglioni's, though neither was to be seen. An oddity; the midget was never far from his master yet now there was no sign of him. As there had been none during the fight when, surely, a bodyguard would have felt his charge needed protection.

A fact Dumarest noted as he moved to stare through the open doors. Mirza had gone, taking her rafts with her, her guns, her dead and hurt. Now the valley lay in shrouded darkness, the glow of starlight broken by the brilliant streaks from the firebirds, the fan of brilliance spilling from the open portal, diminishing as the panels closed to seal the house as it was before.

"Earl?" Govinda was beside him. "Earl?"

She looked lovelier than ever, the mane of her hair a cascade of flame, the lines of her body delineated by the close-fitting gown she wore. One which left her shoulders bare, her arms, revealing the long, silken curve of her thigh at every other step.

"I was worried, Earl," she said. "When Mharl hit you I felt my heart move as if it would burst. Then, when you didn't go down, I knew you would be victorious."

Had she been watching? Dumarest frowned, trying to remember, but Mharl had demanded all his attention and she could have stayed in the shadows.

"Tama was worried too," she said. "I sensed it. As I sensed how that old bitch felt toward you after you'd won. At that moment she would willingly have made you her equal had that been your ambition. It made me jealous." Govinda rested her hand on his arm. "Would you have gone with her had she asked?"

"No."

"Refused the chance to share the power of the Karroum? Do you mean that?"

He said, bluntly, "I'm not in the habit of lying."

"But—"

"It would be power short-lived. No Family would tolerate the introduction of a stranger on such terms. There are too many with too much to lose." A threat settled by the use of an assassin, a subtle poison slipped into food or drink, a convenient accident—there were too many ways of dealing with the unwanted. "Where is Toyanna?"

"What?" The question startled her. "Why, with Tama, I suppose."

"No." He looked to where Chenault stood at one end of the table, leaning against it, using the board to steady his balance. "No, she isn't there."

"Why do you want her?"

"To talk." He smiled at the expression in her eyes. "To share a drink with her. To enjoy her company."

For a moment her face seemed to blur, to become hateful, ugly, then it smoothed and she smiled as she looked up at him, the gleam of her eyes emerald in the shadow of her brows.

"You're teasing me, Earl. Trying to make me jealous. You're not really interested in Toyanna. No more than you are in Hilary. Not as a woman, that is. Not as someone you need to hold close."

"Need?"

"Need." Her voice lowered as she repeated the word. "There is an ache inside of you which has lasted too long. A yearning for something you once had and hope to have again. Can you deny it?" Then, as he remained silent, she laughed and moved away. "Perhaps you will find it, Earl. Stranger things have happened."

She moved on, passing the group at the table, the servants attending them, becoming a blur as she blended in with the decor of the hall. The circus adornment he had seen before; the bars and cages and visage of clowns. The smoldering colors, the bizarre and fanciful decorations. Symbolism he could appreciate and a message which was plain; he had been accepted by the others of the entourage of Chenault. Tama Chenault who had once owned a circus—and the circus took care of its own.

"A happy ending." Chenault nodded a greeting as Dumarest joined him at the table. "A difficult situation neatly solved. For that you have my gratitude; I have no wish to be enemies with the Karroum."

"Gratitude." Dumarest helped himself to wine. "Is that all?"

"I don't understand."

"Words are only vibrations of the air. The cheapest form of repayment there is. From you, Chenault, I want more."

"Such as?"

"You know the answer to that. The reason I came to see you. When are you going to give me what you promised?"

"Soon." Chenault lifted his goblet, wine rilling to stain his chin. "It will be soon."

"Tomorrow?"

"I think so. Yes. Tomorrow."

"I'll anticipate the meeting." Dumarest took the goblet from Chenault's hand, refilled it, handed it back. "A toast, my friend. To life!"

"To life!"

Again wine stained Chenault's chin, the goblet shattering as he lowered his hand. Dumarest reached for a cloth but Toetzer was before him, a napkin busy as it soaked up the wine. If the hand had been cut there was no trace but the red wine could have masked any blood.

"You must pardon me." Chenault swayed a little as he straightened. "Stress and fatigue together with my recent indisposition—I'm sure you understand. A momentary weakness but I think it best to retire. Jem, please attend me." He turned as he neared the side of the hall, Toetzer at his side. "Goodnight all." He waved his hand at the assembly. "I bid you all good night."

As he left the hall Massak turned to Dumarest, smiling. "Well, Earl, what now?"

They gambled, one against the other, elbows to the table, biceps straining as each tried to force the other's hand to the board. Mercenary's fun with a candle glowing to give added incentive to win. A game Dumarest had played often enough with glowing coals instead of candles and, at times, the bared steel of a naked point. A hard game for hard men and he guessed why Massak insisted on playing it.

"You're hard, Earl." Massak rubbed the back of his hand. "Hard and fast and as tricky as they come. The kind of man good to have at your back when the trouble starts. Once more for luck? Double or quits?"

"Try it with someone else."

"I can beat them all. Even Shior." A man hurt with a dislocated shoulder; the last of his targets had been alerted and had fought back. Now Shior rested in drugged slumber and Massak was impatient to regain his eminence. "Once more, Earl. I insist."

And, losing, would be sullen. Dumarest knew the type too well and, even if he beat the man, would gain nothing from his victory. Yet to yield was not enough; like the mistress of the Karroum, the mercenary had his own concept of honor.

"The last time, then." Dumarest took his place at the table. "Double or quits."

"As you say." Teeth flashed white as Massak grinned. "The candles, Tyner." He waited as flames rose from the wicks Lopakhin kindled. "Now!"

A surge and he had thrown all his strength into the combat. Dumarest felt his arm begin to yield and fought back, not to win but to give the illusion of a hard-won battle. A moment of strain and, slowly, Massak's hand was forced back, to stand almost upright, to bend slowly toward the other side. Sweat shone on his face as, baring his teeth, he resisted the pressure, forcing Dumarest's arm back, back, bending it until the back of his hand hung over the leaping flame of the candle.

Lifting as Dumarest fought back.

Falling again to hover as hair singed and the flame licked flesh. A guttering flare which died as Massak forced the hand to quench the wick.

"I won!" His roar of triumph filled the hall. "By God, I won!"

"Try him with knives!" Toetzer, returned, yelled the challenge. "Face him with naked steel and I'll give you odds of twenty to one."

"No!" Dumarest was curt.

"Why not?" Elated by his victory Massak was eager for combat. "First blood, Earl. Just a touch to decide who is the better man."

A single cut which would lead to others and to final maiming or gory death. A combat without reason, profit or cause. Dumarest recognized this but knew he could never get Massak to accept. The mercenary was too much a barbarian for such logic and, his blood heated, wanted nothing but to fight.

"Wait!" Dumarest looked at the ring which had formed, the avid faces. "You want a battle, right? Then we'll give it to you. Here!" Steel flashed as he drew his knife and sent it to quiver, point in the board, halfway down the table. "You at the far end, Ian. Jem, give us full goblets." Dumarest lifted his own, Massak doing likewise. "We drink and go for the blade. Who'll give the word?"

"I will!" Toetzer shouted down the others. "You ready? Go!"

Dumarest sipped his wine, threw the goblet and its contents at Massak, was down the table and gripping the freed knife before the mercenary guessed what was happening. His roar of anger echoed from the roof.

"You cheated! By God, you cheated!"

"Did I say we were to drink it all?" Dumarest sheathed the knife, smiling, one hand falling on Massak's shoulder in apparent friendship. "If you can't win fair, my friend, then you have to win foul." In a lower tone he added, "Stop this before one of us winds up dead."

And Massak had no doubt as to who that would be. The shower of wine had sobered him, that and the sight of the naked blade, the face of the man who had held it pointed at his throat. Death had been close then and he knew it. Knew too that Dumarest, by cheating, had given him an out.

One he took as, laughing, he clapped his own hand on Dumarest's shoulder and called for wine to celebrate a draw.

"To the finest companion any fighter could hope to find. One hard, fast, cunning—and who can take a joke." He lifted his goblet. "To Dumarest!"

That toast was followed by others and it was late when Dumarest finally made his way to his room. His head ached a little though he was far from drunk, having pretended to drink far more than he had actually swallowed. Under the cold sting of the shower he thought of Massak and how he had left him; swaying, bawling mercenary songs and reliving old campaigns. A man who could

107

have been an enemy but who now swore he was a friend. As Mirza Karroum had done. As Chenault had promised to keep his word.

The spray ceased and Dumarest stepped from the shower to dry himself and, killing the lights, lay naked on the bed. Starglow from the window filled the room with silver, making a screen of the ceiling on which he projected mental images. Chenault standing in the clearing, tall, silent, almost as if graven from stone. Chenault in the hall leaning against the table as if for support. The same man who had rilled wine over his chin. Who had smashed a goblet in his hand.

His face had been the same as it had in the study before his attack. His body, even his stance, but had there been a subtle wrongness? A man affected by drugs would have acted as he had done, a little unsteady on his feet, a shade unaware. Had Toyanna doped him so as to make a necessary appearance when Mirz had arrived with her demands? And, if she had, would he be fit enough to tell what he knew about Earth?

A worry accompanied by another: if Avro was still alive then his personal danger was very real. He could have guided the woman to him—but no, the last thing he would want was for her to take her revenge. Instead he would use other methods and Dumarest never made the mistake of underestimating the power of the Cyclan.

He dozed, starting awake to a faint rattle from the door, the sound as of someone trying to get into the room. Rising, he jerked away the chair holding it fast and opened the panel. In the passage outside Govinda shrank from the glittering menace of his knife.

"Earl! I—"

"Come inside." The door closed behind her, the chair again rammed into place. "What do you want?"

A stupid question; the answer was in her eyes, her face. In the heat of her body felt as she stepped close to him. In the message of her arms as they lifted to close around his neck.

In the burning demand of the kiss she imprinted on his lips.

"I love you," she whispered. "Earl, my darling, I love you."

He said nothing, the knife hanging at his side, his free hand rising to caress her hair.

"Since the moment I saw you I knew we belonged together. I can sense such things. As I sense the void in your heart. The space you ache to fill." The pressure of her body was a warm and succulent invitation. "A space I can fill, my darling. My dearest darling. My love!"

A woman enraptured, enamored, hopelessly in love—or one pretending to be.

"Hold me, Earl! Take me in your arms, my darling. Kiss me! Kiss me!"

Words to excite the senses, and gestures to match but all were the province of every actress and even the most inexperienced harlot knew how to emulate passion. Again he caressed her hair, running his hand over the contours of her body, finding nothing but heated flesh beneath the gossamer thinness of her robe. Yet weapons could be hidden in unsuspected places; drugs placed beneath the nails could bring quick unconsciousness once their points had pricked the skin and an ampoule, crushed between the teeth, could vent numbing vapors when impelled by a kiss.

Yet she had kissed and touched him and he was unharmed.

"Earl, what is wrong?" She stepped back from him, eyes wide, luminous in the starlight. Dark pools of shining brilliance as her hair was dark in the starglow. As were her lips and nails and darting tongue. As the thin fabric of her robe which showed betraying glints as she moved. As the dark areolas of her nipples surmounting the breasts which shifted with wanton, unfettered abandon. "Earl?"

The magic was too strong. The web spun by perfume and starglow and warm, feminine flesh. Of soft lips and yielding contours and the ache in his heart which she seemed to know too well and which never ceased to hurt. The pain of what had been and would never be again. Could never be again until the end of time.

"Earl?"

"No!" He moved, reaching for the light, his head turned from her, eyes blinking, narrowing at the sudden, warmly yellow glare. "Don't say anything. Just leave me. Just—" He turned, falling silent as, around him, his universe collapsed.

"Earl!" Kalin stepped toward him, arms lifted, mouth curved as he had seen it curve so often, eyes filled by the light he had never thought to see again. "Earl, my darling. My very own wonderful darling!"

An illusion. Govinda using her talent and making herself appear to him as the thing he most wanted to see. The woman he most ached to possess. The one he missed most of all—and now had found again.

Had found again!

The joy of it blazed through him as he folded her in his arms. The touch of her lips, her hands, her body banishing all thought of illusion from his mind. She was what he wanted her to be and, becoming it, made him see her in that guise. See her and love her as he had never stopped loving her.

"My darling! My love!" She cried out in the bittersweet pain of his caress. "My love!"

Later, when again starglow filled the room, Dumarest turned to where she lay beside him, seeing the cascade of her hair spread on the pillow not black as it seemed but flaming red as he remembered. As red as the flame which she had set to burning within his heart.

In the dimness the lights were like the eyes of watching insects; red, yellow, blue, green, flashing and changing even as Kooga watched. The telltales on the instruments he had added; extra monitors which even now recorded every variation of the electromagnetic fields of the cyber's brain. Among them Avro lay like a corpse, mummified, immobile. The oxygen which kept him alive now pumped directly into his bloodstream by the mechanism which had bypassed both heart and lungs.

A man, dying as all men must die, but the manner of his passing was something novel to Kooga's experience. The vitality was incredible as if, like an animal, the cyber clung to existence against all odds. And, as he sank even deeper toward final extinction, the cerebral activity increased against all logic. The patterns recorded by the pens of the encephalograph were of a complexity Kooga had never seen before: presenting a puzzle he itched to solve.

"Doctor?"

The nurse had arrived to make her routine check and stood, deferential, waiting for him to clear the area. A good worker, obedient, deft with her hands. Too deft for her to have done what he had told Vaclav she had done; such a nurse would never have disturbed any connection. But the lie had been a facile explanation of what he would rather the Chief did not know.

"Doctor? Shall I attend the patient?"

"A moment." Kooga forced himself to soften his normal, brusque manner. "Have you noticed any change in his condition?"

"None that has not been recorded, Doctor."

"No blame is intended," he said quickly. "I was thinking more of some intuitive feeling you may have had which did not register on the monitors. An impression," he urged. "A personal assessment which you may have felt. Such things

112

happen." Too often for the peace of mind of those dealing with the bricks and mortar of ordinary medicine; sensations which defied analysis, guesses, hunches, odd certainties which led to unexpected results. He added, appealingly, "You know this is a special case and any help you can give will be appreciated."

"I'd like to help, Doctor, it is my duty but—" She paused, frowning. "I don't think I can be of assistance."

"Let me be the judge of that."

"It's just that when I was attending him before the bypass was introduced I had the oddest impression that he was shouting at someone. It was as if—"

"A moment, nurse. Was that after Mirza Karroum paid her visit?"

"Yes, just after you had attached the recorder to the patient's larynx." Her eyes met his, wide, innocent. "I noticed it, of course, while making the routine check. The higg-load light was showing on the encephalograph and, as I touched him, I seemed to hear a voice. Well, not hear it exactly, but—"

"Sense it?"

"Yes." She smiled her thanks at his help. "Almost as if a finger had touched my brain. But not quite that either. It was just a feeling. I can't explain it and, naturally, didn't report it. I'd almost forgotten it until you asked."

A burst of cerebral activity which could have been triggered by her proximity and, because of the subtle affinity with the sick gained during her years of service, she had sensed it with a talent barely suspected. Kooga studied her as she stood beside the bed. An ordinary, honest, hard-working woman with an ingrained deference to those in authority. Questioned by the Cyclan physicians she would repeat what she had said and their questions as to the recorder he would do without. To discharge her would be simple yet that, in itself, could give rise to questions. Good nurses were simply not thrown aside without cause.

He said, "As I remember it, nurse, you are due for a vacation. Certainly you merit a reward for your dedicated service. A month, I think, would not be too long. Starting immediately."

"Doctor?"

He saw her puzzlement and guessed its cause; he was not noted for generosity or undue concern with the welfare of those beneath him. Deliberately he grew brusque.

"Aren't you due for vacation? I must be mistaken. However I am making other arrangements for this patient and you will no longer be needed. I was thinking of the Bilton Resort—you could fill in as emergency medical staff. I owe the resident practitioner a favor and you could help to repay it." To explain too much would be a mistake; one he avoided by an abrupt termination of the subject. "I will make all arrangements. Be ready to leave by morning."

Alone he looked at the figure lying supine on the bed. Closing his eyes he tried to capture the feeling the nurse had mentioned but he lacked her affinity and gained nothing from the experiment. Opening his eyes, he studied the interplay of the telltales, the winking gleams which held a subtle mockery.

The visible signs of cerebral activity of a man with a brain grown too big for his skull. One more dead than alive yet who, if the nurse was correct, was screaming for help.

To whom?

Chapter Eight

Chenault said, "I owe you an apology, Earl. We should have met earlier."

"Two days ago." Dumarest was blunt. "I had your promise."

"I was not allowed to keep it." Chenault lifted his shoulders in a shrug. "At times Toyanna can be a veritable bully and she has the means to enforce her will. However, as I hear it, you have been pleasantly occupied."

With the realization of a dream but Dumarest made no comment, looking instead at the study in which they sat. It was as it had been before; filled with the musty smells of old paper, leather, ancient oils. The repository of things long dead and things he hoped were still alive. On the table before him a decanter of ruby wine threw a warm patch of luminescence on the polished wood.

"Legends," mused Chenault. "Stories from ancient times each holding a grain of truth. Dazym Negaso claims that a legend is, in reality, a means of passing a message from one generation to another. In order to be effective that message has to be simple and repetitious as well as holding its own attraction. So we talk of Eden, a place of ease and plenty. A place in which none knows pain. One in which all needs are satisfied. Things all find enticing. Bonanza is much the same; a world with seas of rare elixirs, mountains of precious metals, plains studded with gems. El Dorado much the same. Jackpot, Lucky Strike, a host of others." Pausing he added, softly, "And, of course, we have Earth."

"Which is no legend."

"As we agreed. The Original Home of Mankind from which they fled because of some devastating catastrophe." Chenault lifted his hands to make a T. "From Terra they fled—"

"Yes," said Dumarest. "We've been through that."

Chenault ignored the interruption, finishing the quotation, then, lifting his hands still in the position he had placed them, added, "The one became the many and the many shall again become the one. This in the fullness of time."

A ritual and Dumarest repeated it.

"You are wise." Chenault lowered his hands. "If we are to learn then we must learn to read

117

what the ancients have left us. One race, leaving
Earth and becoming the multitude of diverse types
we now have. In time they will conjoin to become
one again. This, I think, is clear. What is not is what
they left behind. A planet devastated, destroyed,
deserted—yet you are the living evidence that some
remained. How did they survive? How far have
they shifted from the original norm? What have
they become?''

Dumarest said, bitterly, "Savages."

"You are sure? Remember, you can only speak
from your own experience."

"That and others. I was a boy when I left Earth.
Stowing away on a ship and deserving to be evicted
into space. The captain was kind, he spared me.
He also kept a journal." Dumarest reached into a
pocket and produced a folded sheet of paper.
"Shakira had a sensitive, Melome, who had the
ability to throw a person mentally backward through
time. She managed to get me back in the ship, in
the captain's cabin, looking at his open book. I
read what he had written. This is it."

Chenault took the paper, opened it, read aloud,
" 'The cargo we loaded on Ascanio was spoiled
and had to be unloaded at a total loss. A bad trip
with no prospect of improvement so I took a chance
and risked a journey to the proscribed planet. A
waste of time—the place is a nightmare. God help
the poor devils who lived here. Those remaining
are degenerate scum little more than savage animals.
Found a stowaway after we'd left, a boy who
looks human. He claims to be twelve but looks

younger and could be dangerous. Decided to take a chance and kept him but if he shows any sign of trouble I'll have to—' " Chenault looked at Dumarest. "It ends there."

"I know."

"Were you the boy he mentions?"

"Yes."

"Dangerous," murmured Chenault. "He was right in that but he should have added lucky as well. Not many stowaways are treated so gently. But this is no proof the planet he landed on was Earth."

"I am the proof of that." Dumarest looked at his clenched hand, lifting it to slam hard on the table. "Damn it, man! I know where I was born!"

Silence followed the fading drum-echo of the beaten table, broken by a soft click and, turning, Dumarest saw Baglioni standing before an open panel, one hand buried in a pocket.

"It's all right," said Chenault. "It's quite all right." He smiled at Dumarest as the midget retreated behind the closed door. "I appreciate your impatience, Earl, but we must be objective. The evidence, alone, does not support your contention. Yet, obviously, you must have left the planet of your birth. A ship must have carried you. As you rode with it you must remember its name." He paused, waiting. "Do you?"

"It had more than one name," said Dumarest. A fact he hadn't understood at the time. "When I joined the ship it was the *Cucoco*."

"And the captain?"

119

"Petrovna. Zuba Petrovna."

"You see, we make progress." Chenault gestured to the wine. "Help yourself and relax. A tense mind and body do nothing to help solve any problem. One we can now look at from another angle. During your search you must have found clues. They are?"

The spectrum of the sun which was Earth's primary; the Fraunhofer Lines forming a unique and identifiable pattern. The circle of the constellations forming designs when seen from Earth. A moon resembling a pocked skull when seen in the full. A direction. A region in which the planet must be; one toward the edge of the spiral arm where stars were few and the nights lacking the splendor of Lychen.

Items over which Chenault mused as if he were a jeweler studying gems.

"The spectrum will tell us where we are when we find it but to isolate one from so many stars is a formidable task. One you have tried, perhaps?"

"Yes," said Dumarest. "The cost was prohibitive."

"Understandable and the effort would be wasted if the computer consulted lacked the essential data. As it is missing from the almanacs such a probability is high. The constellations?" A shrug dismissed their immediate value. "Like the spectrum they will only tell us where we are when we get there. The direction; the seventh decant, well, that covers a vast area. As does the bleak night-time sky. The moon is of little more help as many worlds have oddly fashioned satellites. You have more, perhaps?"

"Names," said Dumarest. "Sirius 8.7. Procyon 11.4. Altair 16.5. Epsilon Indi 11.3. Alpha Centauri 4.3." He added, "The numbers are the distances of the stars from Earth's sun."

"Signposts in the sky." Chenault nodded as he considered them. "Valuable data, Earl. A relationship could be established and the central point found. A simple matter of mathematical determination. Surely you must have checked the data?"

Dumarest said, bleakly, "I tried. The stars are not listed."

"Or their names have been changed. Even so, the correlation remains. The seventh decant, you say?" Again Chenault brooded over the data, leaning back in his chair, his eyes like glass as they gleamed with reflected light. "One other thing; the ship on which you left Earth."

"The *Cucoco*?"

"It must have had more than a name. What were its markings?"

A device totally unfamiliar and now almost forgotten. One Dumarest drew with frowning slowness on the paper Chenault pushed toward him.

"This? Are you sure?" Chenault looked up from the paper, rising as Dumarest nodded. "Let me see, now." He moved to a shelf, took down a heavy volume bound in cracked and moldering leather, riffled through the pages to stand, finger on an item. He said, "The clue, Earl. You've given me the final clue. I know where Earth is to be found."

It was something he had dreamed of a thousand times; the occasion when, in answer to his question, he would receive not blank stares or mocking laughter but the affirmative which would signal the end of his quest. The person who knew where his home was to be found. Now, incredibly, he had found him.

Yet he had to be sure. "You mean that?"

"Yes, Earl. I mean it."

Dumarest said, slowly, "I want the truth, Chenault. No guesses, wild assumptions or vague promises. If you know the coordinates set them down on that paper and I'll be in your debt. But if you're toying with me—" He broke off, looking at his hands resting on the table, the fists they made, the knuckles white beneath the skin. "I'm in no mood for games. Not now or ever on that subject. If you don't mean what you say admit it now."

"Or you will kill me?" Chenault read the answer in the face turned toward him, the hard stare of the eyes. "A fair warning, Earl, but unnecessary. I know where Earth is to be found."

"The coordinates—"

"Have yet to be determined." Chenault lifted a hand to still any protest. "It is merely a matter of time. The puzzle is now complete. I promise you I know the answer. I swear it."

His voice carried the truth and Dumarest relaxed. Wine gushed from the decanter as he tipped it over a glass, the ruby fluid like water in his mouth, warming as he refilled the glass, both drinks joining in his stomach to wash away the residue of tension. A time of celebration, the drinks a libation to ancient gods who, at last, had been kind.

"You gave me the final clue." Chenault resumed his chair, the heavy volume to one side on the polished board. "The device was the sigil of the House of Macheng. They operated in the seventh decant, running a fleet of small trading vessels. The *Cucoco* must have been one of them." Pausing, one hand touching the book, he said with an abrupt change of subject, "Did Shakira ever tell you what his specialty was?"

"He had the ability to recognize talent when he saw it. Even when it had still to be developed."

"And mine is the ability to solve puzzles." Chenault stroked the book with a gesture like a caress. "Anagrams, acrostics, crosswords, riddles—all, to me, are difficulties which do not exist. Elaborate incantations containing hidden meanings, jumbled formulae, the mazes in which men try to hide true meaning all yield to my skill. Can you wonder why I turned to harder problems? Using my skill to unravel the truth hidden in legends? Most are just fanciful stories dreamed up by desperate people to provide a modicum of comfort in harsh and bitter times. The promise of pleasure to come in some distant time. Tales taken and embroidered with added glitter to become worlds of vast and incredible riches. Many such worlds are basically the same—Bonanza, Jackpot, Lucky Strike—all sharing the same promise of vast fortunes. Others offer different rewards; ease, health, youth, tranquility but, again, too many bear the same similarities. Eden, Avalon, Elysium, Heaven, Paradise—you understand the point I am making?''

''Legends and the growth of legends,'' said Dumarest. ''One kernel of fact becoming two, four, a dozen. But Earth is no legend.''

''Neither is Ryzam.''

Dumarest reached for the decanter and poured, looking at Chenault, setting aside the wine as the other shook his head.

''Ryzam,'' said Chenault. ''I'll wager you've never heard of it but you must know what it offers. Youth, restored vigor, health, the crippled made whole again, the maimed and the dying given new life. A magic place with a dozen names—give me one.''

''Argentis.''

''Argentis,'' murmured Chenault. ''And Farnese, Djem, Delyon, Mytha, Elagon; the names are legion. But all stem from one and Ryzam is the source. Ryzam, the origin of a score of wonder-worlds, and yet it isn't a world at all. Just a place on a planet which legend has enhanced beyond all recognition. I must go there.''

Dumarest sipped at his wine and said, ''We were talking of Earth.''

''And now we are talking of Ryzam. A fascinating place, Earl, one steeped in legend and fanciful

124

tales but all stemming from undeniable truth. I stumbled on the essential data while pursuing my studies in kindred legends and soon decided that, somehow, various threads had become tangled to present a false whole. Unraveling them took years, isolating pertinent information occupied decades. Then a trader sold me an old log and in it I found the essential clue. As important to the solution as the one you gave me appertaining to Earth. Ryzam,'' Chenault looked at the decanter, the pool of ruby shadow at its foot. ''A place as important to me as Earth is to you. As I said, I must go there.''

Dumarest said, ''Do you know where it is?''

''Yes.''

''Then you'll have no trouble finding it. As I'll have no trouble finding Earth once I have the coordinates.'' Dumarest paused then added, ''The ones you will give me.''

''Give?'' Chenault turned to meet Dumarest's eyes, his own direct. ''Why should I give them to you?''

''In return for the information I gave you. The clue you said was all-important.''

''And what of my years of study? The expense of rare and ancient books? Logs? Charts? A host of kindred data? And my skill—is that of no value? Come, my friend, be reasonable. Surely you don't expect charity?''

The goblet Dumarest was holding quivered a little; the movement betrayed by the shimmer of the wine it held. Carefully he set it down, withdrawing his hand, feeling the polished surface of the table beneath his fingers. Wood which fretted beneath his nails.

"I want those coordinates, Chenault."

"And you shall have them. I swear it. But not as a gift but as a reward justly earned." Chenault made a gesture, smiling, but the iron of his voice matched the cold hardness of his eyes. "Earth, Ryzam, the two sides of a coin. You need to find one and I must go to the other. Help me and I will help you—it is as simple as that."

On the bed Govinda stirred, mumbling, uneasy in her sleep. Standing before the window Dumarest glanced at her then looked again through the pane. In the shadows fire burned as the nocturnal life of the valley followed its normal path. Streaks of color he noted but ignored as again he tasted the bile of angry defeat. To be so close, to have been led to believe so much—then to have the prize he valued so much snatched from his hand to be held at a tantalizing distance.

If the prize existed at all.

A thought which drove him from the window toward the door, halting as Govinda stirred again, mumbling, rearing up to cry his name.

"Earl! Hold me—Earl!"

The fragments of nightmare which he soothed away with gentle hands, feeling the warmth of her body close to him, the silken mane of her hair soft against his cheek. Only when, at last, she was sleeping quietly did he move, easing free the door, opening it, closing it behind him as he moved

126

down the passage. The stairs were deserted, the great hall, the corridors beyond. The study door was firm and he leaned against it before lifting the knife from his boot and driving the steel to disengage the catch. Inside it was black with a smothering darkness, one destroyed as he found the switch and illuminated the room with an even glow.

It was as he had left it, the wine still on the table, the goblets, one clean the other still holding what he had left. The chairs and, close to where Chenault had been sitting, the massive tome he had consulted. Dumarest opened it, finding the paper on which he had drawn the marking adorning the hull of the *Cucoco*. One repeated on a page followed by scant information.

House of Macheng. Traders. Main field of operations 7th Dec. XVB34TYCS23R.

The truth as Chenault had relayed it—the following figures and numbers were probably some condensed coding which told him nothing. Yet, to Chenault, they could hold the secret he had hunted for so long. In which case there would have to be an appendix.

Dumarest lifted the pages, began to riffle them, then halted as, frowning, he looked at the symbols. Many were alike and he studied the one he had inscribed. Loops, bars, slanted lines and yet . . . and yet. . . .

Then, suddenly, he was a child again, crouched shivering behind a dune, staring at the strange vessel lying before him. The open, unguarded port, the daubed symbol plain against the scarred hull.

Not the one he had shown Chenault but one almost like it. One with two extra bars and one less loop. One which he saw lower down on the same page.

Ukmerge Combine. Traders. 7th and 8th Dec. Fringe. BAS92UGSA73C

The same decant—but why had Chenault made such a play on the importance of the clue? One Dumarest now knew to be false. If the code-figures were the heart of the matter then they couldn't have yielded the correct data. Which meant that Chenault had lied as to his knowledge or had known the answer all the time.

Closing the book Dunarest looked around at the tomes, the charts, the latest introductions. Any researcher needed a system to enable him, if no one else, to file and retrieve his discovered information. The computer? A musty folder? One of the ranked books? If the entire program had been reduced to the essential coordinates it could be anywhere.

Dumarest moved to the computer and tapped keys. The screen lit, flared with the negation symbol, went blank again. What he had expected: lacking the operating code the machine refused to obey his command. A folder marked with a crossed circle held nothing but sheaves of closely typed figures. Another contained computer read-outs useless without the cypher-code. A book yielded nothing and was tossed aside. Others followed it. As he reached for a mnemonic cube Dumarest heard the sound of movement and spun, hand falling to knife, staring at Chenault standing at the end of the table.

"Wine, Earl?" He moved the decanter again, the glass rasping over the wood. "I offer it freely—you have no need to steal."

"I'm no thief!"

"No?" Chenault shrugged. "Then why break in here? What did you hope to find?"

"You know damn well what I wanted." Dumarest took a step toward the other man, another, a third. "I warned you not to play games with me. Not to lie."

"I haven't. I—"

"You're using the oldest con trick ever known: sell someone a promise then make them sweat blood for fear of losing what they never had. You tried it on me. Dangled the carrot then demanded the price. All right, I'll pay it. Give me the coordinates and I'm with you every step of the way." His voice deepened to a snarl, matching the savage mask of his face. "Deliver, Chenault. Play it straight. I warned you what would happen if you didn't."

Dumarest moved, jerking to one side as the decanter Chenault held hurtled toward him to splinter against the far wall with a crash of glass. As he lunged for the door the man caught him, gripping with fingers which reached bone, jerking him backwards with savage force. Dumarest twisted, snatched out his knife, drove the blade directly at the massive torso. It struck, grated, slipped from the chest to slash at the arm. The injury had no effect and Dumarest felt hands close around his windpipe.

"Fool!" Chenault tightened his grip. "You fool!"

Dumarest arched his back, drove up his knee, missed the groin and slammed the pommel of his knife hard on the other's forehead. A blow followed by another a little to one side, more as the hands eased their grip and he tore free.

"No!" Chenault backed, hands lifted to protect his face. "No! Please I—" He broke off, slumping, one arm lifting in appeal. "Help. I need—please!"

He caught at the table as Dumarest reached the door, falling to the floor as he dived into the passage. Turning to follow the path Toyanna had taken, halting as, again, Baglioni appeared before him, dart-gun in hand.

"That's enough!" The midget lifted the weapon. "You know you can't beat this so—"

He didn't see the knife Dumarest threw, didn't feel it until it slammed against his weapon and knocked it from his hand. Didn't see him move until, suddenly, he was suspended in the air, his face inches from Dumarest's own.

"Where is he?" Dumarest snarled his impatience and shook the diminutive figure. "Where the hell is he?"

"Who? What—" Baglioni squealed as Dumarest dug fingers into his neck. "Don't!"

"Then take me to him." Dumarest slammed the man to his feet. "Take me to Chenault!"

Chapter Nine

He lay like a mummy in a crystal tomb; a pale shred of humanity festooned with wires and the pipes of a life-support system. His face was drawn, corpse-like, the mask of an ancient time. One shadowed by an elaborate construction of pads and lenses, microphones and receptors. Looking at him Dumarest was reminded of an insect caught and cocooned by a predatory spider. One who came to stand before him, tall, somber in her black.

"You guessed," said Pia Toyanna. "How?"

"He seemed too young for the age he had to be." Dumarest looked at the figure in the transparent cabinet. "And the first time I sat with him in his study I felt there was something wrong. I couldn't hear his heartbeat or sound of breathing. Other things." Small things added to the one big thing his basic nature had recognized; the absence of a living organism. Sitting with Chenault had been like sitting with a machine. "How long?"

"Since shortly after he sold the circus. His health had been bad for a long time and, suddenly, it grew worse. Myositis, myotonia, myasthenia gravis—his muscular system just fell apart. Toward the end he couldn't even lift a finger."

And so the surrogate. The machine shaped like a man which reacted to the amplified impulses caught by the receptors covering Chenault's body. Lying in his box he would see what the machine saw, hear what it heard and, in return, it would move as he wanted to move, say what he wanted to say.

"Vosper built it," she said. "He's an engineering genius and Lopakhin helped. Basically it's just a sophisticated version of a remotely operated mining robot; one using radio to transmit the impulses instead of wires. A machine—but to Tama it is more than life itself."

"And to Baglioni?" Dumarest glanced at the midget where he stood before the door, silent, rigid in his anger. "He used it too, didn't he? When Chenault was too weak to operate it. The time Mirza came, for example, and the master of the house had to show himself."

"How did you know?"

"He was unsteady, unsure of himself and his control was bad. The glass he smashed by too great an application of pressure. The wine he attempted to pour into his mouth and sent to dribble over his chin. Other things. But it was a good try."

"But Baglioni? It could have been anyone."

"You? Hilary? Vosper at times? The rest were accounted for. And only Baglioni was so fiercely protective of Chenault. A return for Tama giving him the opportunity to feel a fully grown man." Dumarest looked at him, then at her. The midget's loyalty was accounted for but what held her to Chenault? The others?

She said, when he asked, "Tama is a good man. We owe him much."

For her the opportunity to stretch her skills to the ultimate, fighting death and decay with everything she had or could get. For Vosper the chance to prove himself a genius and the same for Lopakhin. For Hilary a refuge. For Toetzer the same. For Govinda?

A woman crippled with her need to become a mother. Toyanna shook her head when, bluntly, he asked the question.

"No, Earl, you can't father her child. No man living can do that. She is barren, sterile beyond all hope of ever bearing life. Transplants are rejected. I've put a half-dozen foeti within her womb and all have failed to survive. And yet still she hopes." Her face softened as she looked at him. "Take my warning, Earl, don't fall too deeply in love with her. Remember, she isn't what she seems."

Not to him or to any man but if the illusion was strong enough did the harsh reality matter? What if her hair lacked Kalin's true flame? Her body was not quite identical? Her mind not the savage flame of true affinity he had once known but a shadow of that overwhelming joy? It was there. It existed and against it the ghost of what had been had no chance. This was a woman he could hold in his arms, feel her, possess her, respond to her own passionate demands. And, on the foundation of wanting, grew the substance of fact.

He loved Govinda.

Govinda . . . Kalin . . . Kalinda.

Now, for him, the two were the same.

Baglioni said, "What are you going to do?"

"Do?" Dumarest saw the anxious inquiry in the midget's eyes. "Nothing."

"I don't understand. If it means so little to you then why force your way into here?"

"I wanted the truth," said Dumarest. "And I grew tired of being taken for a fool. I came here to learn something and I think you all know what it is. Chenault swore he could give it to me. He can still give it to me. Once I have it I'll leave."

"With Govinda?" Toyanna fired the question then shook her head as Dumarest nodded. "She won't go with you."

"I'd prefer her to tell me that."

"She'll tell it—her life is tied in with the rest of us. And we are bound to Tama."

"Bound? Held?" Dumarest echoed his impatience. "That mummery at the table? The secret society? The cult? There is nothing mystical about Earth. It is a planet. A world circling a sun. It knows heat and cold and bleakness but there are no ancient sages there, no magicians, no gods. No answers either," he added, "no matter what you may choose to believe. No superior race from which all others sprung. I know. I was born there."

"And so must be a part of that race if ever it existed." Toyanna pressed her point. "Be a child of those who were left. Carrying in your body their genes, their attributes—tell me, Earl, do you regard yourself as normal?"

He said nothing, staring at her, waiting.

"Your speed," she said. "I saw you fight and, at times, you seemed a blur. Such reflexes are rare. And the way you knew Chenault's surrogate was not really a human being—how many ordinary people would have sensed the difference? With Govinda you—but never mind that, enough to say that you have a certain charm which appeals to the basic in a woman. I've felt it, Hilary, even Mirza despite her age. A defensive mechanism, perhaps, certainly a survival trait. For your genes if not for yourself. And there is more. Why are you so enamored with returning to Earth? What attraction can that world have for you? Or is the need to return based on something deeper? A drive dictated by a compulsion beyond your comprehension?"

Questions for which he had no answers but only another question.

"Are you saying that I'm not human?"

"No, not that. If anything you could be more than human. An improvement, taking humanity as we know it, a better breed of person." Toyanna made a gesture of resignation. "As a doctor I've seen too many divergencies from the norm. Any norm we care to establish so that now the word itself has ceased to hold meaning. A man is an animal who can breed with others of his kind. No matter what shape he has, what color, what size—as long as he can breed, he belongs to the same species. Even mutants as long as they remain sexually viable must be termed human no matter how they appear. Even freaks.''

The disfigured and distorted and deranged. Those who drooled and lived in dreams and sloughed their skin as if they had been reptiles. Giants and midgets and women who had found another world within themselves. Artists and fighters and the woman he loved who was not what she seemed and could have no offspring.

Dumarest narrowed his eyes at the thought, wondering if Toyanna had deliberately planted it and why. Was Govinda a mutant who had progressed one step too far? Something which, despite her shape, could no longer be called human?

He said, ''We've talked enough and I've waited too long. Wake Chenault and ask him what I want to know.''

''He's worn out. The effort of your fight weakened him.''

''A few words,'' said Dumarest. ''A few numbers; the coordinates of Earth. Something he can give and lose nothing in the giving. He swore he could help me.''

''He can.''

"Then wake him." Dumarest stepped toward her as she made no move. "Do it!"

"And if I don't?" She added, quickly, "Don't answer that, I can guess. But why?"

"I warned him but he still tried to trick me."

"A fault, but—" She broke off, gesturing at the cabinet. "An old man, weak, dying, afraid, doing the best he could. Wanting to survive and knowing only one way to do it. Needing you as we all need you, Earl. Your speed, strength, courage, determination. Your luck." She met his eyes, his frown. "Yes, Earl, your luck. If we are to succeed we need all we can get."

"For what? Ryzam?" Dumarest thinned his lips with impatient anger. "You want me to join you chasing a fable, is that it? All right. I agree. Give me the coordinates of Earth and I'm with you all the way. That's what I told Chenault. The offer I made. He refused to accept it."

"He could have cheated you. Given you false data."

"He could have tried."

"But you would have made him verify the figures as far as possible. You wouldn't have trusted him. Yet you can't seem to understand why he couldn't trust you. You could have taken the figures and left."

Dumarest said, flatly, "I gave my word."

"One he should have taken, perhaps, but, in his place, would you?" She paused then said, before he could answer, "I promise you this; after we've been to Ryzam he will give you what you want to know. All you want will be yours.''

Or Chenault would be dead and the knowledge he held lost with him. A gamble Dumarest was reluctant to take and yet there seemed to be no choice.

He said, bitterly, ''The old and weak have a strength of their own. All right, tell Chenault he's won. I'll have to trust him—but if he cheats me not even Ryzam will save him.''

On the side of the valley something flashed, died, flashed again. Gleams Dumarest noted, assessing time and direction before running toward the slope, bent low, blending into the vegetation his boots soundless on the loam. Halting to wait, to move again, to make a sudden dart and to lift Govinda high in his arms.

She squirmed, writhing, resisting his grip with spring-steel reaction, relaxing as she recognized him, slumping to lean against him, masking him with her hair, the mounds of her breasts warm against his cheeks.

''Darling!'' She brushed back her hair as he set her down. ''I didn't see you. What were you doing—spying on me?''

''I saw a flash and was curious.''

''About this?'' She lifted a pair of secateurs from the basket which had fallen to one side. Fronds covered the bottom. ''I was collecting herbs. Hilary is going to make a potion for me. Something special. Once you taste it, my darling, you will never leave me.''

"You don't need a potion for that.''

"No?'' Her eyes held his, bright yet vacant of humor, glinting with reflected light as they moved to search his face. "Do you mean that? Would you settle down here with me, grow old with me, spend the rest of your life in this one place so as to be at my side? Would you do that for me, Earl? Would you?''

Massak rescued him from the necessity of an answer. He called up, his voice flat, dampened by the contour of the terrain.

"Earl! Come down here. We need a referee.''

He was stripped to the waist, his torso a mass of ugly scars, livid patches of paler hue which patterned his skin in abstract designs. Shior faced him, also naked to the waist, his hairless chest unmarked.

"A challenge,'' explained the mercenary. "I say Shior isn't fit yet and he claims he is. If he can beat me I'll agree. If he can't then he goes back to his bed.''

Dumarest said, "Fit for what?''

"To live. To fight. To survive.'' Massak shrugged. "Does a man need an excuse for combat?''

"Not an excuse, a reason.'' Dumarest looked at the other man, smaller, slighter built, but equally as dangerous as the mercenary. One now completely healed. "Run to the end of the valley,'' he suggested. "The first to return will be the winner.''

139

"Run?" Massak snorted his disgust. "What kind of combat is that? A warrior does not run."

"Sometimes it pays. Too often a stupidly brave man ends up a dead one."

"True." Shior nodded his agreement. "But some never learn. My thick-headed friend, for one. Even though his scars are a constant reminder. Fire," he explained. "Flame throwers on Appanowitz. I heard the warning and ran but he had to be stubborn. Gambled that he could cut them all down with a laser before they got him. Had there been one less he would have won the bet."

"As it was, Shior had to finish the job and, for me, the war was over." Massak scowled at the memory. "Fire," he muttered. "Those who use it should be roasted over a slow flame. Head-down over a camp fire as we did to the swine who tried to feed us poisoned wine. That was on Amara and it took him a long time to die."

"You fight old wars too often," said Shior. "Come, let's run. The exercise will do you good."

They vanished into the vegetation, Govinda watching them go, shaking her head as the rustling died.

"Men! Always they talk of death and battle and conflict. Why, when there are so many other things to talk about? Small, helpless, loving things to cherish and nurse and watch as they grow to full stature?" Without altering her tone she said, "Have you ever given a woman a child, Earl?"

Dumarest remembered what Toyanna had told

him. "I can't give you what you want, Govinda. No man can."

"Is it so much to ask?" Her eyes, her face, mirrored her pain. "Why when I need it so much? Why must I be denied? Why? Why, Earl? Why?"

The question asked by all born to suffer. By all railing against their fate. Why? Why me? Why?

As always there was no comforting answer.

"You're wrong." She stepped back, shaking her head, chin lifted in sudden defiance. "There is a man who can give me what I need. Tama can. He promised. He swore that everything would be all right. Once we get to Ryzam—" As suddenly as it had come the brave defiance left her and she was weak again, sobbing, broken by the weight of too much yearning, too hopeless a dream. "Earl! Hold me! Tell me it will be all right!"

He obeyed, caressing her hair, holding her close as he murmured words of reassurance. Only when she had calmed did he rise, stooping to pick up her basket, the herbs it contained.

"We'll give them to Hilary," he said. "For that special potion."

"Do I need it?" Her eyes met his and she smiled at what she saw. "Never mind the herbs, Earl. Take me for a walk. To the edge of the valley."

Where the vegetation was thick and the ground soft and the air sweet with the scent of flowers. Where her hair spread in a scarlet mantle on the sward as she lay in the age-old attitude of demanding surrender. Where, afterwards, Dumarest turned

141

to lie supine to stare at the burning vault of the sky through a screen of leaves. Seeing the sun and the tiny mote of the raft which hovered high above the valley like a watching bird of prey.

Vaclav was annoyed and showed it, making no attempt to mask his face as he glared at the image on the screen.

"I'm limited," he said. "I told you that. There's nothing more I can do."

Kooga, equally annoyed, maintained his professional calm. "We had an agreement, Chief. I can't understand why Dumarest isn't in your custody."

"I explained all that. Mirza Karroum has made her peace with him and has withdrawn all accusations. More; she seems to have become his friend. I can't defy the Karroum."

"And Chenault?"

"Alone means little but he also has friends. I can't break into his house to arrest his guest, especially as I've no reason. I've a raft watching the area. If he leaves I'll know it and maybe something can be done."

Justice outraged, his own concept of law turned into a mockery and his office used for personal gain. Things which made a sour taste in his mouth and the fading image on the screen didn't help. Kooga had his own world; one in which he was almost supreme, and the habit of demanding obedience was one which had become a part of his nature. A trait Vaclav found more than irritating and he sat back, glowering at the communicator, his desk, the far wall of his office.

A box in which he had spent too many years of his life.

Kooga had hinted of a means of escape; money to gain independence and freedom from the need of pandering to those who ruled Lychen. The big Families with their whims, their degenerate offspring, their cruelties and unthinking demands. Once he had accepted it and had been glad of the security the Guardians offered. An organization in which he had risen to become its Chief but Luccia had died and their child with her and the driving need to provide for them had ended with their funeral.

A bad time which work had helped to push to the back of his mind, but always their memories lingered, his wife with her youth and beauty and wonderful understanding and the child they had both wanted so much and which had cost so dear.

A drawer opened to reveal their faces; hers still beautiful but traced with lines of strain, the boy's empty, vacuous, a smiling mask which conveyed no humor. A fault in the cerebrum which normal medicine had been unable to cure. A genetic weakness, perhaps. One stemming from the mother but he hadn't been sure and had never wanted to risk repeating the tragedy.

So no wife, no child, just endless work which filled the hours, his only consolation that he was making sure the job was well done.

Now Kooga with his hints and promises and the

growing pressure of his impatience. A man needing a cat's-paw and covering the need with lying
talk of partnership.

Yet, if he was right, one thing at least was true.
Dumarest could provide the escape he yearned to
obtain. The way out if he could stomach the price.

Kooga had no such problems. Dumarest was an
item which Vaclav should have collected by now—
Mirza's change of mind had left the field wide
open. The Chief had the men, the means, the
authority to arrest on his own volition. Why did he
delay? Was he hoping to deal with the Cyclan
direct?

A thought which accompanied him as he left his
office and made his way to the room where Avro
was lying. It was as before; dimmed, the monitors
flashing as they maintained and recorded their
surveillance. On the print-outs the complex pattern
of lines held their own fascination.

Kooga studied them as he had studied the earlier
ones, adding minutes to the hours in which he had
struggled to grasp their meaning. The normal
encephalographic patterns could be ignored; to him
they were as familiar as the fingers of his hand.
But they only formed a background to the pattern
obtained from the cyber. The added lines, their
waverings, their codelike repetitions presented a
mystery he felt on the edge of solving.

Communication?

He felt it had to be that. Comparison with the
words gained by the recorder, matched to the wa-
vering lines, showed a certain correlation. Elemen-

tary cypher-breaking techniques had shown certain positive extensions and a more sophisticated investigation must extend the range of that knowledge. In time, with enough data, he would be able to solve the mystery.

And with it the secret of the power of the Cyclan.

The print-out trembled in Kooga's hands and he let it fall as he indulged in the pursuit of a dream. Power and authority all guaranteed by the Cyclan in return for his silence. A vast medical complex in which his words would be law—and no arrogant bitch like Mirza Karroum would ever again make him feel like dirt.

He looked at the unrolling paper with its mesh of lines. Dumarest was money but this was power and, soon, it would be his.

"Doctor?" He turned, startled, meeting the eyes of the new nurse. "A message, sir. From the Cyclan." She glanced at the silent figure on the bed. "Cyber Zuber will arrive at dawn."

Chapter Ten

Zuber was of his kind; cold, calculating, a stranger to emotion. A living machine who was a physician who had never learned to be a man. The robe he wore was in direct contrast; a warmly glowing scarlet, bearing on its breast the gleaming Seal of the Cyclan. Framed in the thrown-back cowl his head bore the likeness of a skull, hairless, the cheeks sunken, only the deep-set eyes revealing the keen mind within. His hands, his limbs and body, were the parts of a functional machine. Flesh and blood now directed to a single purpose; to serve the organization of which he was a servant.

To Kooga he said, "You have done well, Doctor. At least Cyber Avro is still alive."

"Thanks to your instructions."

"They may have helped but more was needed.

You provided it. Did many help you?" Zuber paused, "There must have been others, surely? Nurses? Assistants? You can be open with me."

Interrogation concealed by courtesy and a continuation of the questioning which had commenced the moment the cyber had entered the hospital with his aides. Men who had vanished on mysterious errands, returning to whisper their reports, moving on about their business. Taking over the patient; Kooga had been refused entry when he had gone to Avro's room. His protest had been met with a facile explanation and he had known better than to argue. Now, and until he was ready, he must act the part of the innocent.

"Was there any unusual occurrence? Anything which could be termed a crisis? Or, if not that, any unusual activity? I mean, of course, in regard to the patient's condition."

"Nothing which has not been reported." Kooga had answered the question before. One differently phrased but identical in meaning. "You have my records and they are complete. Every detail of medication, surgery, dressings, after-care, all are there. A most interesting case but I must confess to feeling relief now that you have taken over. The responsibility was not one I would care to repeat."

"You did your best," said Zuber. "No one could have done more."

And his best had been good enough. Kooga was not deluded by the cyber's compliment or the smooth, even monotone in which it was delivered. One designed to avoid all irritant factors. Had he failed the tone would have been the same even while ordering his death.

Yet he hadn't failed and Zuber seemed satisfied and would soon be gone taking Avro with him. Then he could return to his study of the print-outs, copies of which now lay safely hidden. Work which had occupied him all through the night leaving traces of fatigue stamped on cheeks and eyes.

Details which Zuber had noted and dismissed; men in Kooga's profession were always the victims of weariness.

He said, "There is, however, one small point which I would be gratified if you would explain. According to my information the nurse who tended Cyber Avro has left the hospital by your order. She is now in a distant region. The explanation?"

A shock but Kooga had rehearsed the explanation.

"She was tired. She had worked hard and long and I wanted to avoid the possibility of risk. Nurses get accustomed to routine and tend to lose their fine edge by repetition. They take minor things for granted. Usually such carelessness is unimportant but, in this case—well, I dared not take the chance of an avoidable complication."

"Such as?"

"A change in temperature signaling a potential source of infection. A shift in the position of the patient's body. A stain on a dressing. The malfunction of a monitor." Kooga shrugged. "You know how it is."

Not from personal experience; those who served the Cyclan did not fail, but Zuber could assess the probability. Those subjected to the poison of emotion could never wholly be trusted. Not even Kooga, loyal as he seemed, could be above suspicion. Why had the nurse been sent so far? Why hadn't it been included in the report—his aides had discovered the move while making a thorough check. What had Kooga to hide?

Nothing, perhaps, and yet Zuber knew that the smallest scrap of data could have unsuspected importance. That to ignore it would be to betray a lack of efficiency.

He said, "Regarding the monitors—it seems you went to extreme lengths in order to obtain the most detailed information. Especially as revealed by the encephalograph."

"I assumed you would want me to obtain such data." Fear made Kooga curt. "If you wish it can be destroyed."

"It is complete?"

"Of course."

"Yet the same system of monitoring was not used throughout. A more sophisticated machine was introduced just after the nurse was removed."

"It may have been." Irritation edged the doctor's tone. Questions as to his conduct, even from the cyber, were unwelcome. "I worked on your behalf and you have said you are satisfied. Now, it seems, you question my professional integrity. I did what I did because I judged it should be done. The result justifies my decision."

"Of course. Did you find the print-outs interesting? Unusual in any way?"

"No." Kooga added, "I didn't study them. The data was for you alone."

A lie and Zuber knew it; no physician would have failed to check for possible deterioration in the cerebrum and no one of Kooga's experience would have failed to note the unusual pattern. Anger and fear had betrayed him and had marked the need to terminate his existence.

"I understand." Zuber nodded as if satisfied. "Just one other thing while we are on the subject and then you will be left in peace. To enjoy your reward," he added. "One you have richly deserved."

"Thank you. The point?"

"There was a slight commotion; a woman insisted on entering Cyber Avro's room. The receptionist recorded the incident. She was not alone."

"No."

"The details?"

A matter he had overlooked and Kooga cursed his forgetfulness. The receptionist had been too efficient—or had the power of the Cyclan cast its shadow before it? How many eyes had been watching him? Checking everything he had done?

"The woman was Mirza Annette Karroum," he said. "The man was Vaclav, Chief of the Guardians. They, that is she, wanted to question Cyber Avro. Naturally I didn't allow it."

"Question?"

"Yes, I don't know the details. I ordered them from the room immediately."

"One of the Karroum?"

"Yes, I—" Kooga hesitated. The cyber would

know of the power held by the Karroum and the other big Families. On worlds such as Lychen such were not ordered as if they were inferiors. "She was stubborn," he admitted. "I had to explain how useless it was to talk to the patient, to get any response. Once she understood that she left."

"Thank you." Zuber rose, extending his hand, the broad ring on his finger gleaming in the light. "I think that will be all."

The administrator was a woman, no longer young, her hair long, graying, dressed in a bun which accentuated the sharpness of her features. A face now marked with the stamp of anxiety.

"I don't understand it," she said. "Doctor Kooga seemed perfectly well when I last saw him. A little tired, perhaps, but that's all. Then, an hour later when I had to go to his room to ask his decision on a matter, he was dead. Naturally I sent for you immediately."

"Why?" Vaclav met her eyes. "Did you suspect a crime?"

The answer lay in the room where Kooga lay sprawled on the floor, one hand extended to where the carpet had been drawn back. Vaclav knelt beside him, sniffing at the pale lips, lifting the lids to examine the glazed eyes. No scent of familiar poisons or traces of familiar drugs but that meant nothing. The room itself told him more: the furnishings were ripped, paintings thrown down from their hangings, the entire place looked as if it had been searched.

By whom?

Vaclav looked at Kooga's extended hand. It lay clenched and, as he forced open the fingers, he found a scrap of paper clutched in them. A fragment from a larger piece which bore the tracery of lines. The paper itself was from a photocopying machine.

The administrator waited outside. To her Vaclav said, "Whom did the doctor see this morning? Cyber Zuber? Anyone else, I mean after his interview with Zuber? No? I see. What time did you see him? The exact time, please. Good. And it was an hour later you called on him?"

"About that, yes."

"And found him like this? Has he been touched? No? Good. That will be all."

"But—" She looked past Vaclav at the body sprawled on the floor."

"Leave him for now." Vaclav stepped back into the room. "I'll let you know when he can be removed."

A man dead, trying to reach for something, but why? The room gave the answer, one Vaclav sensed with his years of experience and, standing, looking around, he read the message it conveyed. Kooga, tired, seeking his bed, entering the room and finding it bearing the marks of an obvious search. If he had hidden anything in it he would have gone immediately to it—and those who had set the trap would have what they wanted.

Vaclav stepped again toward the body. Kooga had died but he bore no sign of an obvious wound. Poison was the logical instrument but how had it been administered? As Vaclav looked at the drawn-back carpet, the reaching hand, he saw the minute spot of reddish brown on the pad of the palm. Something which could have been dirt or a fragment of dried blood.

Straightening he looked at the room. A recorder lay where it had been thrown, tapes scattered around it. He examined them, remembering the one Kooga had played, the gained response of Avro with its whispered directions on where Dumarest could be found. Had he told the cyber of Dumarest? Was the tape still here?

He searched them, reading titles, halting as he found one with a single word. Ardestum—an obvious anagram. He played it, listening again to the whispering voice, then rewound it to hit the erase. If Zuber had killed Kooga to get his hidden papers he wouldn't get this. A small revenge but better than none—the power of the Cyclan would give the cyber immunity of punishment for his crime.

Outside, Vaclav threw the tape into a bin with items waiting for incineration. An assistant collected it as he reached the end of the passage, making his way to Kooga's office. As he entered Zuber turned toward him from where he stood at the desk.

"Chief Vaclav. It is good to meet you. I assume you are here to investigate Doctor Kooga's demise. A regrettable loss. You knew him well?"

153

"No."

"But you had met him. With the Lady Mirza Annette Karroum. You were together in Cyber Avro's room. May I ask why?"

Vaclav said, curtly, "She was unhappy with my report on the death of the previous head of her House. She wanted confirmation from Kooga as to the cause."

"And chose the room of a sick man to conduct her investigation?"

"It happened that way. Naturally Kooga wasn't pleased."

"But he answered her?"

"He satisfied her, yes. Now, if you will excuse me, I've work to get on with."

"Of course," Zuber's hand appeared from the wide sleeve of his robe, the ring glowing on his finger. "I must not delay you. I have little time to spare either. We must be leaving soon."

On the ship in which they had arrived, taking Avro with them, his inert body wrapped in a cryogenic sac and frozen against the ravages of time. To be transshipped and sent to Cyclan Headquarters there to be wakened, tested, probed so as to gain every scrap of information from his body and mind. The direct order of Marle, Cyber Prime, who, like all of his kind, abhorred waste.

"I wish you a safe journey."

"Thank you, Chief." The ring glinted as Zuber moved his hand to touch Vaclav's own. "And I wish you success."

The desk was void of anything of value, the

office the same and, back in his own, Vaclav sat brooding on what he had learned. Kooga dead, murdered for something he had possessed. Papers taken from where they had been hidden; copies of something the Cyclan wanted to remain a secret. The one Dumarest held? No, the tape hadn't been taken and so, obviously, Kooga hadn't mentioned it. And the questions Zuber had asked—why had he been so interested in who had been in Avro's room?

A pattern had to be present and Vaclav strove to find it, scowling as the communicator hummed, reaching out to hit the button, his hand freezing as he saw the tiny fleck on his skin.

Something which could have been dirt or a fragment of dried blood.

A match to the one he'd found on Kooga—and Kooga was dead. The communicator hummed again but he ignored it, thinking, remembering. Zuber and his ring and the way he had reached out to touch hands in a farewell gesture. One alien to his breed; cybers did not entertain emotional ceremony. An act, then, to get within range and Vaclav was no stranger to rings which were not as they seemed. A touch of anaesthetic to numb the pain of the dart which penetrated the skin to instill its poison and the thing was done. A man dead but not knowing it, walking, talking, smiling even as the delayed action drug did its work.

How much time did he have?

Kooga had died within an hour after the administrator had seen him but he could have fallen min-

utes after reaching his room. How long before that
had he met Zuber? A computation which carried a
bleak answer—time was short and getting shorter.

Vaclav reached for the communicator, killing
the incoming call, his hand pausing as it rested on
the keys. Perhaps the Cyclan could save him,
neutralizing the poison, and the bribe of Dumarest
could persuade them to do it. But he had destroyed
the tape and had no proof. They would need to
check and that would take time he didn't have. But
if he could talk fast enough and be persuasive
enough—.

A desperate hope and a futile one. Vaclav recognized it as he withdrew his hand from the communicator. No matter what was promised his life
was still forfeit. Knowing of Dumarest and his
value to the Cyclan they would assume he knew
the secret he held. And he had been in the room
with the others. Avro's room with the mysterious
knowledge it held which must never be revealed.
The reason for Kooga's death and his own. Two
out of three with only Mirza left.

Soon the bitch too would be dead!

A moment of gratification then it vanished in a
deeper anger. She was what she was but the cybers
were something else. Killers without emotion,
manipulators, devoid of mercy or tolerance or
sensitivity. Using death as a convenient instrument.
Red swine who had taken his life. To cheat them
was now his only revenge.

The communicator beckoned but he rose; who
knew what tendrils might lie in his department? It

was better to play it safe and he left the office, the building, moving quickly down the street to a public phone. Punching the number, snarling at the delay, curt in his demand when, finally, the screen came to life.

"Get me Mirza Karroum!"

"But—"

"Get her, damn you! Chief Vaclav here! Move!" A pause, a time of nothingness, then her face appeared, hard, cold, impatient. "Listen!" He spoke before she could protest. "Kooga's dead and I'm dying. You could be next." He told her why. "They know nothing about Dumarest but they want him. He could be an ally. In any case you need to watch yourself. Agents could be left to take care of you."

A girl brushed past him as he left the booth, young, well-made, with wanton, inviting eyes. A sight he ignored, looking instead at the street, the houses, the traffic, the bowl of the sky which covered all. Things more precious now than ever before and he drank them as if to store memories against another time.

How long?

The curse of knowledge which all men had but most managed to forget. The fact of inevitable death but, for him, it was close. Reaching for him at this very moment, touching him, causing a shiver to run up his spine. Had Kooga sensed what was happening? Known, too late, that he was dying? Would there be time for him to reach the grave where his love lay buried?

157

He began to walk, faster, faster, breaking into a run. To halt as the light seemed to flicker. To fall as it died.

In their way the Cyclan had been kind. There was no pain, no terror, just a soft darkness on which two faces were portrayed in a golden light. Luccia's and next to her the boy. Smiling as she was smiling, as he had always smiled but, now, there was no emptiness in his eyes.

The valley looked different than it had before but then it had been night and now it was bright with the glory of a dying day. Beauty Mirza Karroum did not appreciate and she sent the raft down to land with a jar which shook her teeth. At the door Chenault was waiting, hand lifted in greeting, a salutation she ignored, brushing past him into the hall.

"You made good time," he said, following her. "I didn't really expect you until tomorrow."

"Where's Dumarest?"

"With some of the others in—"

"Send him out here to me." She glared her impatience. "Now. We must talk in private."

"He's busy."

"And I've no time to waste. What I have to tell him is important. He won't thank you for delaying our meeting. Now move, man! Move!"

She prowled the hall, trying to gain comfort from what she saw; rocks and boulders and writhing streaks of mineral color all forming the illusion of an entrancing grotto. But it didn't appeal and she turned as Dumarest came toward her, hands lifting as if to embrace him, lowering as she realized the incongruity of the gesture.

She said, bluntly, "You're in danger. The Cyclan has men on Lychen."

He said nothing but she saw the slight tensing of his body; the reactive response of nerve and muscle as if he had readied himself for a fight. Things another would have missed but she noted them as she sensed the subtle change in his attitude. Before the news he had been a man tall, calm, smiling a greeting. Now he was an animal, sharply aware, questing with mind and sinew the danger he recognized.

"They came for Avro," she explained. "He told me where to find you."

"How?" He nodded as she explained. "And?"

"Kooga's dead. Vaclav too. Cardiac failure so they said but I don't believe them. Both were murdered. Vaclav knew he was going to die and warned me to be careful. He thought I was to be the next victim. He suggested that you could be an ally."

He said, "Do they know I'm here?"

"No. Not unless Avro's told them and I can't think he did. He was in a coma and will be in a cryogenic sac by now. Vaclav destroyed the evidence. They don't know you're here, Earl." Pausing, she added, "Not yet."

Two words which told him the situation and he looked at her, seeing the hard face, the eyes to match, the rigid line of chin and jaw. A woman almost twice his age and one determined to survive.

"Betraying me to the Cyclan won't help you," he said. "You'd still follow the others and for the same reason. As a precaution against your talking to others about something you may have learned about the Cyclan."

"But there's nothing! I swear it!" She fought to remain calm. "But I can never prove that and they'll never take my word. Earl! What can I do?"

"Run."

"What?"

"Leave Lychen. Travel to other worlds and keep moving. Get lost if you can. Trust no one and say nothing. Make no commitments, no friends, have no ambitions. Learn to be always alone." His voice was bitter from personal experience. "In time they might accept the fact that you know nothing and call off the chase. If you stay here you're dead. Tomorrow, next week, the month after—the Cyclan never gives up."

"But if you were with me? Guarding me?" She saw his expression and shook her head as she recognized the impossibility of gaining total protection. "No. It wouldn't work. You're right, Earl, I'll have to run—but you come with me."

"I can't."

"I don't want to betray you but—"

"I can't," he said again. "I'm going with Chenault. An expedition. There's no point in arguing. I'm going."

"I'll come with you." She had spoken on impulse but it made sense. "Where's Chenault?"

He sat alone in a room bright with flowers, papers scattered on the table before him, a pile of books to one side. Old books which filled the air with the scent of dust and dulled the sweetness of the blooms.

He frowned as he heard Mirza's demand.

"No."

"Why not? I can help. How did you intend to travel?"

"I've a ship."

"Where? What? Your own working as a trader or one you intend to charter? Whatever it is I've a better one waiting on the field at this moment. The *Kasse*. I can have it ready to leave by midnight."

"I won't be ready by then."

"Get ready. What do you need? Supplies? Goods? Weapons? Give me a list and I'll have them loaded from the Karroum warehouse. Damn it, man, why do you hesitate? I've the ship, the supplies, the crew—"

"No crew," said Chenault. "I'll use my own."

"Why? Who do you have?" She glanced at Dumarest then back at Chenault. "What's the mystery?"

Dumarest waited then, as the silence lengthened, he said, "Tell her."

"No. She—no!"

"We're hunting a legend," said Dumarest. "Chasing a ghost. One we may never find but the search itself will be rewarding enough." He saw by her expression she had grasped his meaning. "And the sooner we go the better. Time is against us. It could be fatal to wait too long." Another message but this time with meaning to Chenault also. "I think it would be stupid not to take advantage of what has been offered. Others may think so too. If they do the search is over before it begins."

Mirza said, "And you, Earl?"

"If you go then I go with you." One way to escape the trap Lychen had become and, while they were together, he was safe from her betrayal. "Tomorrow, you said?"

"No!" Chenault slammed his fist on the table. "You can't! We have an agreement!"

"One based on mutual help. The two sides of a coin, remember? I help you and you help me—but what help are you stuck in a chair? How long am I supposed to wait?"

"If you leave me you'll lose—"

"Nothing." Dumarest was harsh. "I lose nothing —you can't lose what you've never had. It's your decision, Chenault. Make up your mind."

He leaned forward across the table with a face the other remembered. One he had seen before when steel had flashed at his torso to cut the artificial flesh of his arm. The face of a killer attacking a machine but one just as willing to attack the man behind it. One too dangerous to be frustrated for long.

"All right." Chenault voiced his surrender. "She can come with us."

"Good. I'll order the *Kasse* to be readied for

flight." Mirza glanced at Dumarest. "Give me a list of what we'll need. And we'll use my crew—I don't trust amateurs in the Burdinnion. Where are we heading?"

"Ryzam. It's a place on a world somewhere. Chenault knows where it is."

"So do I. It's Skedaka on the far edge of the Burdinnion." She looked from one to the other. "Are you serious? Is that the ghost you're hunting? The legend of Ryzam?"

Dumarest said, bitterly, "The place of eternal youth. Of endless health and vitality and all the rest of it. Now you say it's a matter of common knowledge."

"Not common, but it's known. By spacers and traders and those who live on Skedaka. A lot of people have tried to find it." She paused, looking at them both. "A lot of people," she repeated. "But none who reached it has ever returned."

Chapter Eleven

Captain Lauter was a broad, thick-set man, old, experienced, loyal to the Karroum, more than loyal to Mirza Annette. From the depths of his big pilot's chair he lifted a hand to point at the screen before him.

"There," he said. "Skedaka."

A world which was a child of death; seared, torn, gouged, warped by the tremendous cataclysm which had created the Burdinnion. Standing beside the chair Dumarest studied the image set against the background of stars. One which seemed disfigured, diseased, blotched and mottled with drab colors.

"Where's the Ryzam?"

"There." Again Lauter pointed. "That patch to the north."

The image swelled as he increased the magnification, growing to almost fill the screen, the patch looking like a crusted scab on leprous flesh. One composed of soaring spires, jagged, edged with sawlike serrations as if rock had been rendered molten then flung upwards to solidify in flight to form a pattern resembling the gigantic bristles of a monstrous brush.

"You can't land on it," said Lauter. "No clear space for one thing and the forces which stream from it for another. Get to within a certain height and the generators fail. Some ships tried it. None came back."

"None?"

Lauter said, dryly, "It happens about five miles up. When the ships hit the ground—" He clapped his hands together, the sound sharp in the control room. "We'll have to find a spot well clear of the area."

A good spot and a safe one; Lauter had a high regard for his vessel. Dumarest watched as the image shifted, shrank to normal size, looking forlorn and alone in the bright immensity of the cosmos.

"You've been here before, Captain?"

"Yes."

"Then you've heard of the legend. Do you believe in it?"

"No."

"Why not?"

"Because I'm not a fool." Lauter was blunt. "Ryzam is unusual, that I'll admit, but so are a

165

thousand other places on as many worlds. Most of them have legends, tales, stories invented in taverns and spread by the credulous. Usually it's because the natives want to encourage tourists and the money they bring. Expeditions, even. Skedaka is no different. People live there, poor devils trying to scratch a living from dirt that's mostly ash. Sometimes they find gems and rare metals and there's a kind of herb which grows wild. Maybe the legend grew from that—the stuff can give energy and tighten the skin so as to reduce wrinkles. Instant youth. It doesn't last though no one down there will admit that. They have a vested interest in maintaining the legend. In the town they'll sell you everything you need to explore Ryzam. Maps, guns, everything. Sell," he repeated. "They never hire."

"Because no one ever comes back?"

"That's right."

"Do you know why?"

For answer Lauter magnified the image again, this time larger than before, the scab shown in greater detail, accentuating its bleak harshness.

"A maze," said the captain. "Go into it and it's certain you'll get lost. No food. No water. There could be predators and God alone knows what else. The only thing you can be sure of is that there's nothing to find. I guess, when the searchers realize that, they've passed the point of no return."

A facile answer; one to be expected from a man who had spent his life in the ordered confines of a ship, the predictable regions of space. Yet Chenault with his dream was just as bad; his obsession blinding him to what could be an obvious explanation.

He sat in the salon of the vessel together with Mirza and the others; Toetzer, Lopakhin, Massak, Shior. Hilary was with Govinda, and Toyanna, together with Baglioni, was in the cabin holding the casket. Working at the major task of keeping Chenault alive while, in the salon, he planned the next steps of the operation.

"We shall land to the north," he said. "Opposite to the town. The section we want is marked by a cluster of spires resembling a pair of lifted hands. We must pass between them to a space shaped like a star."

Massak said, "And then?"

"Once we have reached it I'll give further instructions as to direction."

"No." Dumarest stepped into the room and up to the table at which the others sat. "That isn't good enough. So far we've followed you blind but no longer. I want to know why you think you can succeed when so many others have failed."

"Because I have information they lacked." Chenault rested his hand on the papers before him. "Ryzam is a mystery, a trap for the unwary, as events have proved. But one man found the solution to the problem and set it down in his journal. I have the relevant passages from it here. Lydo Agutter was an educated and knowledgeable man. I say 'was' but the chances are that he is still alive.

He discovered the truth and set the details down in his book. I have them here."

Shior said, "The secret of eternal life?"

"Yes."

"If he found it why didn't he sell it?" Mirza snapped the question. "Such a secret would have made him rich enough to buy a world."

"Money." Toetzer echoed his disgust. "There are more things in the universe than the lust for wealth. If Agutter were intelligent he would know that."

Dumarest said, "How old is the information?"

"Two centuries at least." Chenault lifted a hand to silence any protest. "Time is meaningless when compared to immortality."

"True, but in a couple of hundred years things can change." Massak voiced the obvious. "Even if he did find the way how can we be certain it's still open?"

"We can't," admitted Chenault. "But knowing it exists gives us the vital clue as to the necessary direction. We follow his instructions, circumnavigate any obstacles, regain the given route as soon as possible. With the talents among us it should be simple."

Talents? Dumarest glanced around the table. Shior and Massak to provide protection with their fighting skills. Vosper, now asleep, and Lopakhin to maintain the surrogate. Toetzer? A sensitive of some kind as was Hilary to warn of danger or discern the correct direction. Toyanna to keep Chenault alive. Baglioni to act as personal bodyguard. Govinda a magnet he couldn't resist. Mirza a passenger and himself?

"You will be in charge, Earl." Chenault adjusted his papers. "When we land you will take over the expedition."

The cabin was small, dark, full of ghostly whispers; the transmitted sounds of activity vibrated through the stanchions, decks and hull. Noise no living ship in space was ever without and one which served as a background to his thoughts. Dumarest turned on the narrow bunk, turned again, feeling metal against his temple, the ghost-sound growing louder, fading as he moved away.

Rising he snapped on the lights and stood breathing deeply before stepping into the mist-shower. The thin spray cooled his flesh and, dressed, he left the cabin and walked down the passage outside. Doors flanked it; cabins holding sleeping figures, one more important than the rest. Dumarest tested it, found it locked, tapped and waited.

"Earl?" Pia Toyanna looked at him through the open door. "Is something wrong?"

"Maybe. Can we talk?" He saw the movement of her eyes and stared beyond her to where Chenault rested in his casket. "Inside? Can he hear us?"

"He's asleep." She stepped back, closing the door as he stepped into the cabin, locking it behind him. "What is it?"

Dumarest looked around before answering. The cabin was much larger than his own, one adapted for its special occupant, a clutter of medical apparatus lying close to the casket itself. A cot near it showed the recent imprint of a body, Toyanna's he guessed, and the puffiness of her eyes told of her fatigue and recently broken sleep.

"I'm sorry if I woke you but—"

"That doesn't matter." She was impatient. "Get to the point."

"Can Tama stand the journey?"

"What?"

"The expedition. He intends to accompany us. Personally, I mean, not just his surrogate." Dumarest glanced to where the machine rested in a chair, slumped a little, looking like a corpse. "Is he strong enough to survive?"

"Yes, if—" She broke off, confused, then said, with a rush, "He isn't as old as he looks. The muscular dystrophy has weakened him but his vital signs are strong and, aside from fatigue, he is in no worse condition than when we left Lychen."

Dumarest said, bluntly, "Don't misunderstand me. I don't give a damn whether he lives or dies but he has something he promised to give me. I want to be sure he has it."

"He has."

"Tell me how you are so sure."

"You gave him the names of stars and their distances from Earth. The names have changed but their relationship remains the same. A box enclosing Earth's primary. It is a simple matter of association to find that box and, when you do, the coordinates of Earth are revealed. And there are other clues which lead to the inescapable—"

"He knows," said Dumarest. "He knows how to find Earth. He knew it long before we met." He read the admission in her eyes. "Why, wanting to reach Earth as he does, didn't he go there?"

"Like this?" She glanced at the casket, the figure it contained. "Look at him. He can't stand. He can't walk. He needs help even to talk. He can barely open his eyes. Yes, he knows where Earth is to be found, but the discovery came too late. Can you appreciate the irony of it?" Her voice grew brittle with emotion. "At times the Gods are more than cruel. They give but demand too high a price. For him it was the culmination of a lifetime of searching—a dream he could never enjoy."

Not unless the secret of Ryzam could be found and he could be made young again and strong and able to walk with pride on the Mother World he considered Earth to be.

Dumarest slowed as he neared his cabin, hearing movement from within, slamming open the door to stare at the woman on his bunk.

"I've been waiting." Govinda threw back the scarlet mane of her hair. Framed by the tresses, her face held an aching familiarity. "I want to talk to you, Earl. Why am I to be left behind with the ship while that old bitch is going with you?"

"A matter of policy." Dumarest crossed the cabin to sit beside her, taking her hands in his own. "We can't always do everything together. Sometimes we have to part as we did that time on Chron. You remember—" He saw the puzzlement in her eyes and changed the subject. The way she

171

appeared to him was familiar as if time itself had folded back on itself, but the memories they shared were limited to recent events. "Mirza insisted," he explained. "She may be old but she's tough and can handle herself."

"She wants to be with you."

"I'm glad of it." He softened the admission with a smile. "While she's with me I'll have no fear of the ship leaving us stranded. And, if you're with the ship, I'll have no fear of losing you, my darling." His hand reached out to touch her hair, her cheek, the smooth line of her throat. "Don't you know how much I care for you?"

"Show me!"

A demand he couldn't refuse and for a time the cabin became a palace filled with wondrous delights and the murmurs of their passion added strength to the ghost-sounds roving the vessel.

"Earl!" Her hand was the warm caress of a kitten. "I love you, my darling. Always remember that I love you."

"For ever and ever?"

"Until the end of time. Earl, my darling, I swear it! I've never felt this way before. I can't imagine life without you. Please be careful."

"I will."

"Ryzam!" She shuddered in his arms. "A death-trap. Everyone says so. Even if you find what you're looking for you'll never come back. I'll be alone again. Alone. Earl, how can I bear to be without you? How can I live?"

Fears he soothed with soft words and gentle

caresses until, exhausted, she fell asleep in his arms. A warm, soft and yielding bundle of feminine loveliness. A woman who was all he could ever hope to find. One reborn, resurrected, more precious to him than anything in the universe aside from the one thing which dominated his life.

Ryzam could provide it.

Once Chenault had solved its secret and had gained what he was after Dumarest would finally learn where Earth was to be found.

The *Kasse* landed at dawn as near to Ryzam as Lauter could manage, and an hour before noon the expedition was on its way.

From his position in the lead raft Dumarest looked back at the others strung out in line to the rear. One, the third, was bulked with Chenault's casket, the surrogate itself, Toyanna and Baglioni who, armed and grotesque in his armor, looked like a malevolent gnome from some tale of an ancient time.

Behind them, at the rear, Hilary rode with Shior and Vosper together with supplies of food, water and other essentials for survival. Toetzer and Massak held second place. Mirza and Lopakhin completed the complement of the lead vehicle.

All wore mercenary combat armor complete with air tanks and radio communication. All were armed.

"It's like an army." Mirza turned to look back at the line. "I've seen pictures like this in old books. Men wearing metal casings and going out to fight. They looked like machines and I guess we look the same.''

"Killing machines," said Lopakhin. He leaned forward to gain a better view of what lay before them. ''And there's another.'' He gestured at the forest of bleak and serrated spires now clear in the russet light of a sullen sun. ''There it is, Earl. A graveyard if ever I saw one. Let's hope to God we don't add to its reputation.''

"Men don't die without reason." Dumarest adjusted the controls and sent the raft higher, watching to see if those following did likewise. ''And we can't be sure that no one has ever come back. Maybe they did and decided not to talk about it. Or, if they did, their stories never got around.''

''Or they found the secret and wanted to keep it for themselves.'' Mirza turned to face forward, her machine rifle falling to clash on the side of the raft as the sling slipped from her shoulder. ''Damn! Sorry, Earl!''

"Is it cocked?"

''No. I'm not that stupid. I told you I knew how to handle these things.''

The truth and he hoped the others had been as honest. Shior and Massak placed among them would provide a steadying influence and yield fast action if it was needed. Chenault was another matter. His casket was fitted with antigrav units for easy handling but nothing could lessen its bulk. If an attack came the other rafts would provide covering fire.

Details settled on long before the *Kasse* had landed and put into operation with the minimum of delay. Ryzam was too harsh, too foreboding to be contemplated for long without imaginary fears rising to augment any real dangers. And those, if they existed, were still unknown.

"An army," mused Lopakhin. "You'd think a force like this could go in and search and find whatever is to be found. Given enough men and firepower who could stop it? That's what makes nonsense of most legends. If the lure is strong enough the truth will be found. Even curiosity will do it. Any problem which—" He broke off pointing. "Earl! Quick! There!"

"What did you see?"

"Movement. Something—" Lopakhin shook his head. "It's gone now."

Dumarest searched the area and saw nothing. An illusion, perhaps, one born of the light and shadow and an active imagination. Even so he tripped the radio switch within his helmet.

"Movement reported directly ahead," he said. "Can anyone verify?" His listened to the chorus of negatives. "All right. It was probably a trick of the light. We'll lift another hundred yards."

The height would betray them to a greater number of watchers if any existed but gave a sense of comfort to those unaccustomed to the dangers of the unknown. As the sun passed its zenith they neared a configuration of spires which held the vague likeness of a pair of uplifted hands.

"There!" Chenault was triumphant. "The hands Agutter mentioned. Beyond will lie the star."

The beginning of the journey discovered in the

old journal and Dumarest hoped it would be as uneventful as the trip so far.

Mirza voiced his suspicions. "It's too easy," she said. "Just fly in and land and then keep moving. I don't like it."

Dumarest made no comment, eyes narrowed as he stared ahead. Ryzam was beneath them now, the area ringing the edge and, he guessed, relatively harmless. But to plunge on would be to invite destruction.

"All rafts halt," he said into the radio. "Massak, Shior, bracket Chenault between you. I'm going ahead to see what's waiting. Keep alert." To the others in the raft with him he said, "Keep watch to either side. If anything comes at us shoot."

He sent the vehicle rising, aware of the turbulence which must exist close to the sun-warmed spires, the danger of being swept against their serrated edges. As it moved forward he searched the crevasses, most shrouded in shadows cast by the spires, haunts of mystery and menace. On, the configuration of hands passing to one side. Farther, the star-shaped clearing a splotch of relative brightness; then, as it drew level, he felt the raft lurch beneath his hands.

"Earl!"

He heard Mirza's cry, ignoring it as he fought to maintain height, the raft wheeling as it fell, tilting, Lopakhin shouting his fear as he was thrown against and over the edge. A clutching hand saved him, fingers which caught in the straps restraining the supplies and he hauled himself back into the body of the vehicle as it juddered, veering to drop as Dumarest sent it back the way it had come. A fall which threatened to send them hard against the spires to be impaled by the jagged peaks then, abruptly, the vehicle was alive again and heading up and out from the heart of Ryzam.

"God!" Lopakhin was sweating within his helmet. "I looked at death just then. What the hell happened?"

"No power. Something cut the engine." Dumarest cautiously tested the controls. "It's all right now."

"A fault?" Mirza thinned her lips. "These rafts were supposed to have been checked."

"They were." Dumarest glanced at the handlike spires as they fell to the rear. "Captain Lauter told me of a force which comes from Ryzam. Something which cuts out ship generators. It must affect rafts the same way."

"So we can't just fly in." Lopakhin grunted. "It's obvious when you think about it. If rafts worked Ryzam would be mapped and charted by now. So what now, Earl? Do we walk?"

"Not all the way." Dumarest spoke into the radio telling the others what had happened. "Come in to meet me, Shior. We'll unload, move back out and transship the supplies. Chenault comes in last."

"What about the rafts?"

"They stay outside. All but one. Let's get moving!"

The uplifted spires rose to enfold them with a symbolic embrace, one too like a grasping prison

177

to be comfortable. The star-shaped clearing was smooth, the seven pointed rays set equally at the circumference of the central space. There they landed to stack the supplies. By mid-afternoon it was done, only Chenault waiting for transshipment.

"I'll get him." Dumarest climbed into the sole remaining raft. "Take over, Ian. Set guards and keep everyone on combat alert."

Massak saluted. "You expect trouble? Here?"

"Everywhere. Keep the women among the bales and have men watch from every angle." Dumarest glanced at the surrounding spires, their bases wreathed in thickening shadows. "Stay put. No exploring. We shouldn't be long."

A wind had risen by the time he reached Chenault, small dunes piling against the sides of the grounded rafts. Chenault himself, impatient, looked at the lowering sun.

"We're wasting time," he complained. "This shift could have been completed in one move."

"We can afford wasted time," said Dumarest. "We can't afford mistakes." He glanced at Toyanna and jerked his head. She followed him to one side out of earshot of the others. "Tell me something," he said. "Can Tama operate his surrogate by a cable?"

"Yes. Why?"

"It could be necessary. One other thing, the midget stays behind."

"I can see why," she admitted. "But he won't like it."

Baglioni was furious. "No. I refuse. You can't make me."

"You stay." Dumarest was firm, then softening his tone, explained. "I'm leaving two rafts here, one under the hands and the other in the clearing. There'll be a gun in each. We may have to come out in a hurry and we'll need all the help we can get. The raft, the guns, someone to come to the rescue. That's you, Baglioni. You're the best suited." He allowed of no argument. "Pia, follow me in your raft to the hands and pick me up. I'll ride with you to the clearing."

Where the camp had been set and death was waiting.

Chapter Twelve

It came as the dying sun gilded the tips of the spires and Chenault was busy probing the star rays for signs Agutter may have left behind. A search as yet barren and which would have created disappointment in an ordinary man but which only caused him to move faster as he touched and scanned the walls. Toetzer had joined him, Shior following as if by accident. It was Hilary who screamed the warning.

"Look out! Danger! Be careful!"

Then, the harshly strident blasting of a gun.

Shior had been fast, reacting by instinct, firing at something he hadn't recognized. A broad, disc-like creature edged with scrabbling legs which dropped from the side of a spire to land and rear with snapping mandibles. A thing six feet across, two thick, armoured like a crab, the carapace the dull hue of the spire on which it had lurked.

One followed by others, a flood as it died beneath a storm of shattering lead.

"Helmets! Close helmets!" Dumarest snapped the order into the radio as he snatched up a gun. Vapors could be emitted by the things, acid sprays, numbing gases—in Ryzam no possibility could be ignored. "Massak! Guard the women! The rest of you—move!"

They advanced behind a hail of bullets which smashed through armor, spilling greenish ichor, pulpy flesh, oddly shaped organs. A curtain of protection from which Chenault stumbled, Toetzer following, Shior standing to cover their retreat. An act which cost him his life.

Dumarest saw the movement as, again, Hilary screamed a warning. Things seeming to peel from the spires, falling to land, scrabbling, rearing, darting forward with startling speed. Swamping the lone figure, muffling the blast of his gun, absorbing the missiles Dumarest poured into them.

"Hui!" Massak roared his anger. "Those damned things! They've got him!"

Tearing through his armor with mandibles like shears. Ripping at the soft flesh exposed beneath the protection. Feeding on his body and blood.

"Back!" Dumarest caught the mercenary and threw him toward the bales. "Hold your position. All of you! Back! Back, I say! Back!"

He fired again, a long burst which emptied the clip, sending more broken and shattered disc-things to join the others twitching on the ground. Reloading he looked at the spires, seeing them flake into new creatures which glided down to join the feast. Tearing into their injured fellows with savage ferocity. Cannibalism common among all such predators living in a hostile environment.

"We must press on." Chenault lifted a hand, pointing. "I thought I saw Agutter's sign down there."

"We can't." Dumarest fired again, a short burst which sent broken things twitching to one side. "There must be millions of them. They coat the spires. Waiting dormant until aroused." He fired again adding, grimly, "They're waking now."

There were too many to kill and he knew it. Already they must fill the crevasses behind them, blocking off the path to the hands, the edge of Ryzam. The raft couldn't carry them all and it would take too long to return with the others. The only hope of survival was to keep the creatures away from them. To hide their scent and presence.

"Cease fire! Freeze! Seal your suits!" Dumarest snarled as Vosper continued to fire. "Obey, damn you! Obey or I'll gun you down!"

Movement had attracted their notice and the scent of water vapor expelled from lungs and sweat had brought the things in for the kill. Shior's death had provided irresistible bait. Sealed the suits would prevent the smell of water escaping and, while motionless, the small party could ape the rocks, the lifeless surround.

"Lice." Toetzer echoed his disgust. "Like a

swarm of lice. Vermin lusting to feed. Fruit of evil and degeneracy and the instrument of vengeance against those—"

"Shut up, Jem!" Hilary was sharp. "This is no time for you to start preaching."

Massak, more practical, said, "What now, Earl?"

Dumarest studied the situation. The creatures had fed, those replete now clinging to the rock, blending into it, their carapaces, he guessed, absorbing the weak energy from the sun. Others, still questing for food and water, had slowed and would soon again become dormant. The sun, lowering, would be giving less energy and, with darkness, the things would probably enter some kind of brief hibernation.

But the night could bring other perils less easily seen and combatted.

"Tama, move slowly and check on that sign you saw." The surrogate, a machine and not a man, needed no armor or suit, yielding no attractive scent. Only its movement could bring unwelcome attention. "Don't go too far and freeze if anything shows an interest. The rest of you rip open the bales. Load up with food and water. Set extra containers to one side. Toyanna, pick those you want to carry the casket." Dumarest waited, then, into the radio, said, "Tama?"

"There's an opening. A wide crack, narrow at the top, fretted at the bottom. Debris is lying around. I think some of your bullets must have shattered a wall of some kind." Chenault added, "Agutter's sign is to one side and above it."

183

The path they needed to take if the old instructions were valid.

Dumarest said, "All of you get ready to move. Head for that opening. You stay with me, Toetzer. Massak, you cover the rear. Ready? Move!"

He stood, waiting, Toetzer at his side, a pile of cans of water at their feet. Before them gaped the mouth of a ray leading from the clearing, one of the seven points forming the star. It lay opposite the one with the opening. As the column crossed the clearing and the creatures began to stir Dumarest picked up one of the cans.

"Now, Jem. Do as I do. Throw them as far as you can."

The container left his hands, thrown with all the power of back and shoulder muscles, hitting to bounce and slide deeper into the opening. Another, a third, Toetzer's falling short. He gave a strangled cry and, without warning, ran after it, snatching it from the rock, unsealing it before hurling it from him in a rain of glittering droplets.

"Feed, you spawn of hell! Drink the blood of man and give him the fruit of his earned torment! Drink, you vileness and filth of degeneracy!"

"Come back, you fool! Back!"

Dumarest snatched up his gun, its blast cutting short the sound of the thin, insane babble coming from the speakers. Bullets ripped into the other containers and smashed racing creatures into twitching pulp. As Toetzer came stumbling toward him Dumarest backed, following the others.

"Here, Earl!" Massak was beside him, gun blasting flame. "He'll never make it."

A judgment based on experience. Toetzer was too far, moving too slowly, falling as they watched to be covered with a mass of ravenous creatures. His screams echoed from the speakers, dying as the two men fired and continued to fire until the creatures and the man were dead, unfeeling flesh.

Firing again as they backed into the opening to bring rock showering down from the roof. A barrier Dumarest sealed with a final burst then, satisfied, turned to look at a cavern of nightmare.

There was a glow in it, a pale luminescence stemming from things which hung like elongated fruit from points high on the walls and roof. Others glowed lower down, some of different shapes from the others, some, as he watched, appearing to twitch.

"Bunch up," he ordered. "Keep a sharp watch— you women watch the roof."

He studied the floor as they moved forward to where the cavern narrowed to a gaping tunnel. It was littered with debris, scraps and fragments of darkish brown material, the sheen of broken metal, shreds of what could have been plastic. The residue of earlier inhabitants or those who had followed Agutter's path. As he neared one of the glowing bundles it moved, bobbing on its stem, jerking as if it contained something alive and struggling to escape.

As Massak lifted his gun Dumarest said, sharply, "No. Don't fire."

"It could be dangerous."

"It is, but not yet. We were lucky. My guess is that whatever is inside those sacs sealed the wall. Maybe in order to breed. Later we'd have been their food."

To be taken, cocooned, planted with eggs which would hatch to devour the helpless, paralyzed prey. Now, replete, the creatures were ready to break free, open the wall and stream like a tide after new prey. A cycle, repeated endlessly, life living on life. The normal way of nature but in Ryzam so concentrated as to defy understanding.

The tunnel held more of the sacs, their number diminishing, to be replaced with masses of softly glowing fungi in a variety of convoluted shapes. A fairyland of deceptive beauty through which Chenault led the way, brushing strands from his lenses, stirring dust with his shoes.

"It's hot!" Mirza voiced what they all felt. "God! I'm roasting!"

The heat increased as they progressed, wending their way along and down a winding slope, breaking out into a vaulted cavern to pause beside a cairn bearing an eroded can.

"Agutter's!" Chenault snatched at it, lifted the paper it contained. Reading he said, "To those who have followed me so far—congratulations! The path now lies to the left. At the next cairn it will be safe to rest."

As he turned to follow the directions Dumarest said, "Hilary? Is it safe?"

"I can't be sure." Her voice echoed her indecision. "I sense something but I'm not sure what. Toetzer could have told you—he had an ability to sense inimical forces. I—I wish he was here."

But the man was dead, paying for his insanity, his skills now lost to the expedition. As the party moved on Massak stepped beside Dumarest, resting his gloved hand on his helmet, the fingers tapping in a signal he recognized.

"What is it?" Dumarest put the question after he had switched off his microphone and had touched helmets to form a conductive link. "Something worrying you?"

"A lot of things, that cairn for one. Why should Agutter have left a message? If he was going in how would he know where it was safe to rest? If he was coming out how the hell did he get through those creatures?"

Questions Dumarest had already considered. "Things could have been different then. Anyway, what choice do we have?"

"None, I guess." The mercenary grunted his acceptance of the situation. "But, if it comes to it, we stand together, right?"

"We all stand together."

"Sure, unless—well, you know what I mean." Massak swore as sweat stung his eyes. "This damned heat! It isn't natural. If it gets worse we'll have to take off the suits."

That would mean walking comparatively naked

187

E. C. Tubb

in a realm of unknown dangers advertising their presence with every step.

"We'll wait," said Dumarest. "We can stand a lot more of this."

Vosper couldn't.

He walked at the front of Chenault's casket, guiding it together with Lopakhin at the rear, stumbling at times, his breathing harsh within his helmet, loud over the speakers. Watching the roof, the walls, checking their rear, Dumarest didn't see him lift his hands to raise the visor and expose his face to the air of the cavern. Only his voice, breathing his relief, told of his action.

"By God, that's better! I was burning in there, the air searing my lungs, but this is sweet. Try it. All of you, try it. Hilary. Mirza. How about you, Tyner? Keep this up and you'll run to melted lard."

"Better that than what you're risking."

"An artist voicing his fear." Vosper was mocking. "Admitting he's a coward. Open your helmet, man. Taste what fresh air is like. It'll open your mind. You'll be able to create a masterpiece when we get back. A vision of unsurpassed beauty to stun the eyes of men. And women, too, naturally." He broke off to giggle. "It's like wine. The air, I mean. I've never felt so good."

Totanna said, warningly, "Earl, he sounds as if he's been drugged."

"From the air?"

"What could be carried in it. Those fungi could

shed spores and many types produce hallucinogens. I think you should make him reseal his suit."

"You could try it." Vosper laughed as if delighted at the prospect of amusement. "But you'd have to kill me to do it. Want to try, Earl? You, Massak? Maybe the two of you could manage it. Maybe we'd all die in the attempt. Stupid, isn't it? Here we are, looking for eternal life, and we're talking about killing each other. No need for that. Just leave me alone. I'll be all right."

A possibility, already his voice was gaining its normal sobriety and the impact of what could be in the air might have passed. Certainly it was too late to prevent any damage and, if the air was harmless, it was well to know.

"Earl?" Toyanna again. "What shall we do?"

"Leave him."

"But—"

"Just leave him."

The rest moved on into the depths of the cavern, to where tunnels gaped, to the one on the left which led to a long gallery crusted with distorted figures of stone glowing with the pale sheen of organic decay. To a place where the floor was gouged as if by mighty claws and walking was difficult.

They camped when they could go no farther, sleeping in sacs inflated and washed clean by tanked air. Stripping to lie close as Dumarest and Massak shared the watches sitting alone in the brooding stillness of a world beneath a world.

*   *   *

There had been no cairn. Chenault looked at the hand Dumarest extended toward him, then, slowly, produced the paper he'd found in the eroded can.

Reading it Dumarest said, "I can go no farther. May God help all poor fools who search for an empty dream. If any find this be warned and think of Samu Lowski." Folding the sheet he handed it back. "You lied."

"Can you blame me? How far would any of you have gone after reading this?"

"As far as we've come now. Too far, perhaps." Dumarest looked at the sacs, those within. Awake now, eating from cans, drinking, easing their bodies. "You could have picked a stronger team."

"I took what I could get." Chenault dismissed the subject. "We're here now and must make the best of it. The source can't be too far—Ryzam isn't that large. If it lies at the center a few more days should do it. Less if we have no trouble."

And, after they found it, they would have to get out.

A problem Dumarest ignored; worrying about future difficulties made them no less.

He said, "How are you? Physically, I mean."

"I can manage."

"That isn't what I asked. You should conserve your strength. What are the coordinates of Earth?"

"They're—" Chenault broke off his near-automatic response. "No. Not yet. I'll give then to you when we find what we're looking for."

They pressed on, suffering from weariness of previous effort, the debilitating effect of heat and the dehydration it caused. The helmets were open now; Vosper's continued good health having proved the safety of the air, but still the enervating heat remained. Lopakhin provided the explanation.

"It must be due to hysteresis. Look." He waved his gun violently in the air and held it out for Dumarest to touch. The metal was uncomfortably warm. "We must be cutting through lines of force of some kind. That generates the heat."

"At our speed?"

"I know, Earl. It's unusual. Normally it needs a high velocity but, apparently, not in Ryzam." The artist shrugged. "All I can suggest is that we remove the suits."

A suggestion followed, the weight and bulk tucked in a niche to be retrieved on their return. A pragmatic arrangement: if they could survive the journey in they should be able to survive it out. Massak marked the spot with a daub of paint sprayed from a can, lifted it, smiling, sent more to mark the wall higher up.

"I've used it all along," he explained. "I've been in caverns before and once fought an engagement in an underground installation. I got lost then and if it hadn't been for someone with more brains I'd have died. He used wire to mark the path but paint is just as good."

An elementary precaution and Dumarest had taken it but his markings had been more subtle. If any of the group panicked and wanted to run he didn't intend to provide them with an easy path to follow. Now, more than ever, safety lay in numbers.

The column had lengthened a little, stretching as difference in strides accumulated to create gaps and openings. Dumarest called a halt, bunching them close, moving forward to check what lay ahead. The vast gallery they had been following changed to a vaulted cavern with low-sweeping roofs, curved walls, a floor which undulated like a rolling ocean. It levelled as it ran beneath a convex roof cracked, pitted and scarred with crater-like blotches. The air held an acrid, acid smell which caught at his nostrils. The glow from the rock was dimmer than that they had passed.

"Wait!" Hilary caught his arm as he returned. She stood with her head tilted a little as if she heard things silent to others. "Up ahead," she whispered. "I sense it." Her voice rose, the scream chopped off by Dumarest's hand.

"Danger?" He spoke softly into her ear. "Like that you sensed before in the clearing?" He felt her nod. "From above?"

"I can't be sure." She gasped as he uncovered her mouth. "It's just that I know something's going to happen. Something bad."

Lying in wait somewhere in the area ahead. When it struck, Vosper died.

It happened quickly; a blur which ended at his throat to become a thing of nightmare, scaled, spined, the shears of mandibles tearing at his throat. A spider-like thing two feet across swinging on a thread from a crater in the roof. More followed it, bodies which jerked to the impact of bullets to hang broken, spinning like grotesque ornaments on the end of glistening threads.

"Run!" Dumarest barked the order as he fired. "Get clear of this roof! Massak! Mutual cover!"

He ran to the wall behind him, dropped, crouching, gun lifted to blast in rapid but aimed fire at the menace from above. The mercenary followed, both men firing to protect the other, the rest around the casket. A trained maneuver free of the danger of panic-firing and the wildly aimed bullets which could deal unintentional death.

Bodies fell between them to lie twitching on the ground, mandibles tearing at oozing flesh, the creatures feeding as they died.

Hilary screamed, screamed again, the sound ended by the blast of a gun. Mirza shouted curses as she cleared the air above the casket. Running, firing, Dumarest and the mercenary joined the others as they reached the far side of the area. Pulp and ooze marred the transparent surface of the casket. Blood at the throat of the tattooed woman. It jetted through Toyanna's fingers as, looking at Dumarest, she shook her head.

"Hilary!" Lopakhin dropped to his knees beside her, blood on his cheek, more streaming from a lacerated scalp. "Please, for God's sake—"

"Tyner." Her hand rose to touch his cheek. "You're hurt, my dearest. I'm sorry. I didn't want to leave you. But I'm so tired. So very . . ."

Her voice faded, dying as she died and for a moment there was silence. Then the artist rose, gun in his hands, tears streaming down his cheeks as he emptied the magazine at the craters blotching the roof, the lurking horrors they contained.

Chapter Thirteen

Dumarest turned, gun lifting, lowering as he recognized the woman coming toward him. He sat with his back against solid rock, beneath a roof barely eight feet from the ground. A branch cavern and a safe place for the camp.

"Mind if I join you, Earl?" Mirza Karroum sat as he gestured to the spot at his side. "I couldn't sleep," she explained. "Too many thoughts, I guess."

Accompanied by too many worries. It had been three days since Hilary had died and she looked what she was; an old, tired, disheartened woman. She needed the consolation he could give.

He said, "You should ask Pia to give you something."

"To make me sleep? No. Would you?"

"I'm working."

"You're always working." She looked at him as he sat limned against the glowing rock. A man naked but for shorts and boots; the protective mesh of his own clothing had forced him to discard it because of generated heat. "On guard. Keeping watch. Pushing us all and keeping us a unit. Chenault couldn't have found a better man."

"He needs to rest."

"He's dying." She was blunt. "Pia tries to hide it but I know the truth. He's drawing too deeply on his reserves. Maybe he won't make it. Maybe none of us will."

"We knew that from the beginning."

"Ture, but still we came. The lure of a dream." She stretched out her hands, turning them to show the brown blotches on the skin. Her left wrist bore a scarlet tattoo. "The brand of the Karroum." She had noticed his interest. "It's applied as soon as possible after birth. To avoid any substitution. Angado had one—you must have seen it."

"His wrist was scarred."

"Then he must have had it removed. He never did like his heritage." With a gesture she dismissed the subject. "Why did you join this expedition, Earl?"

"Chenault has something I want. Why did you?"

"I told you—the lure of a dream." Again she extended her hands. "Look at them, Earl. Old like me. Ugly as I am ugly. As I've always been ugly. They used to laugh at me when I was young, not to my face for I was of the Karroum, but behind my back. Somehow it seemed more cruel that way. Then, when I grew older, I could see pity in their eyes. Pity!''

She turned her head and Dumarest waited, saying nothing. When she faced him again she had regained her composure.

"I looked too much like a man so I acted the man and became harder than one, more feared, more hated. But I was born a woman, Earl, and I want to be one. A young and beautiful woman. One whom some man would love.'' For a moment she looked at her hands, strong, square, the fingers blunt, spatulate. "I'd follow Chenault to hell if he could promise me that.''

"You have.''

"Yes.'' She leaned back, pleased with his answer, glad that he hadn't tried to lie to her, to soften the truth she knew too well. "And so far I've been lucky. Hilary wasn't. Neither were Vosper, Shior—''

Dumarest said, sharply, "Don't count the dead.''

"Why not? Superstition?''

"Just don't count them. They are gone. The living remain.''

"To be cherished, cared for, guarded, loved.'' She was bitter. "I've heard that before, somewhere. From a mercenary. A man blinded by a laser—for a while he was my lover.'' She paused as if expecting comment then, when none came, she said, "That was a lie, Earl. If it was true what would you think?''

"That you were kind.''

"To give a cripple the use of my body?"

"To have given a man in need the pleasure of being wanted."

"And that is important?" She answered her own question. "What could be more important? To be wanted, needed, loved. Did you guess that Hilary and Lopakhin were lovers? That he felt so deeply about her. Tell me, Earl, if it had been Govinda who had died would you have shot the spiders or Chenault?"

"He didn't say it would be easy."

"No, he didn't, but if we find what we're looking for and get back alive will you bring her down here to gain what she most needs? Do you love her enough for that?"

"You doubt I love her?"

"Govinda? No. That is obvious to all with eyes. But is your love big enough to include a child of her body? Could you share her with a baby?"

Dumarest met her eyes then, smiling, said, "There's an old recipe on how to cook a meat pie. It begins—"

"First catch your animal. I know. I'm sorry, Earl, at times I ask too many questions." Her hand reached out to rest on his own. "But I warn you, if I get what I'm after, your lady could have a fight on her hands."

"You flatter me."

"Is the truth ever that?" For a moment her hand lingered with unmistakable warmth then, as if annoyed at having betrayed herself, she lifted it to gesture at the cavern around them. "The Karroum own mines. I inspected them once and learned something of geology. I've been studying these fissures and galleries and, to me, they seem wrong. Almost artificial as if formed by some unnatural process.''

"As if something had weakened the crust of this world to release the magma,'' said Dumarest. "To let it fume upward in a fountain of bubbles and froth.''

"Which cooled too quickly. You've noticed that? The surface formation is unique in my experience and is geologically impossible. No natural eruption or weathering could ever produce such a configuration.''

"And the glow?''

"Natural minerals within the rock which fluoresce to the impact of radiation.'' She added, "It could be the same force which produces the hysteresis. Lopakhin told me about it. He also noticed that the glow isn't steady; it fades then brightens again. The deeper into the caverns we go the more pronounced the change becomes.''

"Which means we're getting closer to the source of energy.'' Dumarest had observed the change. "One which pulses but I've not been able to establish its rhythm. There could be peaks and valleys. Times when this entire region could be almost dark and others when it might be filled with destructive energy.''

"A mystery,'' she said. "One to add to the rest. Why no attacks since Hilary died? We could have passed through the habitable environment of Ryzam but, somehow, I doubt it. My skin crawls too much and too often. As if something is watching me. Waiting for me to get closer. You've hunted?''

Dumarest nodded.

"Then you know what I mean. A predator has its territory and it waits until its prey is within reach. When it is it strikes.'' Her hand slapped against her thigh with a flat, meaty sound. "We've had it too easy since Hilary went and it worries me.''

"You'd rather be fighting for your life?''

"We do that every second of every day in one way or another. No. I want to see my enemy. The thing which gave Ryzam its reputation. We could turn round and go back and, with luck, make it to the rafts and on to the ship. If we've met all the dangers we could return with men and flame-throwers. Armored domes, machines, drills to blast an opening from the surface. It would take money, yes, but if the reward is high enough the money could be found. So what lies ahead, Earl? What is it that, once found, can never be left?

In the lead Chenault lifted his arm. "There,'' he said. "There . . . there . . . there. . . .''

The words slowed, slurred as the surrogate took a step, the manlike figure staggering, remaining upright to lean against the wall. Touching it Dumarest found the synthetic skin warmer than it should be. At his side Lopakhin swore as he eased open a panel to release a puff of acrid vapor.

"Heat! I told him not to move this thing too fast! Now he's burned out a junction!''

200

"Can you fix it?"

"I can try but Vosper was the engineer." Lopakhin looked around. They were in a rounded gallery ending in a triple junction of narrower passages. Chenault had pointed to the one on the right. "I'll need room so had better get down to it here. Space could be limited farther on. The light's good, too."

Blazing patches which shone with scintillant brightness to dispel all shadows. At the casket Toyanna was busy checking dials and registers, straightening to look at Dumarest with a worried frown.

"It's all right," he said reassuringly. "Just a shorted connection. It won't take long to repair." He glanced at the casket, the corpselike figure it contained. "How's Tama?"

"Alive—just." She echoed her fear. "But there's something else. The power's going. If the antigrav units fail we'll be stuck unless we can carry the entire weight."

"We can't."

"But—"

"There are five of us not counting the surrogate. One man must stay on board." Which left four to handle the burden, two of them women. Dumarest said, "You'll have to lighten it. Dump all emergency supplies and equipment. You'd better start doing it now. The radio-units can go first; when we move off we'll use a cable to link up the surrogate."

"Tama won't like that. He wants to maintain full mobility in order to guide us."

"He can do that verbally. In any case the surrogate can be put to better use. Get busy now. Stand guard, Mirza. Watch the rear. I'm going ahead to see what's in front of us."

Massak had preceded him. As Dumarest passed into the narrower passage he saw the mercenary standing lower down. He too had stripped to shorts and boots, the scars on his body making a livid tapestry against the rich darkness of his skin.

"Listen!" He held up a hand as Dumarest halted at his side. "Hear it?"

"No."

"Try again. Hard." Massak grunted as Dumarest shook his head. "It's gone now anyway."

"What was it?"

"A sound, high, thin, something like that made by a generator. But it had something extra to it. Something like—" Massak shook his head. "I can't describe it. Maybe it was just imagination." He looked at the passage with its rounded roof and concave floor. "This place can give you all sorts of ideas. Look at it—it's just like a burrow."

One which could have been made by a gigantic worm slithering through plastic magma or grinding its way through rock with adamantine teeth. Fancies enhanced by the silence, the smooth walls, the mounting tension as the party moved along what could easily become a trap.

"If anything comes at us, anything really big, that is, we wouldn't stand a chance." Massak gestured with his gun. "No niches," he explained. "No cracks to duck into. No side passages. We

202

could be caught front and back and turned into pulp.''

"If anything came," agreed Dumarest. "If we couldn't stop it."

"You don't think there's any danger?"

"Not from things as large as you're talking about."

"Maybe not," admitted the mercenary. "Things that big would have to eat and there's damn all around here that I can see. But that brings up another matter—where are all those who came this way before?"

"If any did."

"They must have done if they were following the lure of what's supposed to lie ahead. I've been trying to figure out these caverns and galleries and they seem to me to all be leading to a common point. Maybe Chenault's found a shortcut but, even so, others must have used it. So where are their bodies? Discarded equipment? Supplies? Clothing? We've left enough behind us and others must have done the same."

One, at least, had done more.

Dumarest saw it as they emerged into a vaulted chamber set with patches of brilliance, the mouth of a tunnel gaping opposite the one they had left. Close beside it, set upright against the wall, rested the unmistakable tracery of a skeleton.

"Bones!" Massak stared at the place, gun lifting with automatic reflex in his hand. "Someone died there."

"A woman." Toyanna stepped back after making her examination. "Look at the shape of the pelvis, the set of the thighs. The skull, too, bears feminine characteristics. And yet there's a strangeness about it. As if it wasn't wholly human."

Dumarest said, "Can you tell the age?"

"Of the woman? About middle-age, I'd say."

"No. How long it's been here."

"Impossible." Toyanna's shrug was expressive. "What we're looking at seems to be an imprint of the skeletal structure rather than the bones themselves. Something like a negative print—see how white they are against the dark background?"

Lopakhin said, "I've done work like this. You take an object, a leaf, flower, animal, insect— anything will do. You place it on a prepared and sensitized surface then expose it to a blast of high-intensity radiation. The result is an image of the object but one containing more detail than can normally be seen. A kind of aura." His hand lifted to rest on the stone. "See? This faint blurring following the bones. And here. And here." His fingers moved to halt over the pelvic area. "Could she have been pregnant?"

Toyanna shrugged. "It's possible, I suppose. Why do you ask?"

"This." Lapakhin moved his finger. "See? This part. And this. There's a different kind of shading." His hand dropped to his side as he moved away. "But what killed her?"

Dumarest stirred, waking instantly, one hand reaching for the knife in his boot. Kneeling beside him Massak shook his head.

"No need for that, Earl. Listen."

The air was filled with a thin, high singing sound that wavered, carrying overtones of bells.

"Is this what you heard before?"

"Yes, but it's louder now. Closer." In the dimness the mercenary's face was tense. "Much closer—and it's coming nearer."

Wailing and singing from the air, the stone, the gaping mouth of the tunnel beside which the tracery of the skeleton kept warning guard.

One almost invisible now; the gleaming patches had dulled to somber glows, the chamber gaining a new menace with the loss of illumination. A good place to stay, he'd decided. One in which to check their gear and rest. To sleep as he had slept while Massak had stood watch. As the others were still sleeping.

"Earl?" The wailing, undulating sound had touched the mercenary on the raw. "What the hell is it?"

A question echoed by Mirza Karroum as she woke, eyes bleared, rubbing strength into her sagging cheeks.

"I don't know." Dumarest touched Lopakhin on the shoulder, found Toyanna already alert. "Spread out. Make no sound and don't move. Whatever it is we don't want to attract its attention."

Good advice but not easy to follow. Not when the sound grew louder; shrilling, tinkling, sweet with the music of bells, strong with the whine of generators. Resting his fingers against the casket, Dumarest felt the transparency quiver beneath his touch. Beneath the somnolent figure it contained, a warning lamp began to flash in pulses of red.

"Give me room!" Toyanna had spotted the signal. A panel lifted as Dumarest moved to one side, her fingers deft as she manipulated keys. "His heart," she explained. "If it gets any worse I'll have to introduce a bypass."

"I thought you dumped all nonessential equipment."

"This is essential." She sighed her relief as the red lamp ceased its flashing. "His heart is a muscle too, remember, and as weak as the rest of him. I had to provide for an emergency."

One drowned in the present problem. The singing, chiming, wailing sound which now filled the chamber with demanding noise.

"Look!" Lopakhin pointed. "The skeleton!" The tracery was glowing as if each bone had been delineated in fire. "The light!"

It filled the mouth of the tunnel, eye-bright, scintillating, glowing as if it was made of ice and diamond and cold, cold flame. A writhing something which flowed from the opening to hang in a shimmering mist of glowing radiance. One which shifted, changed, adopted new and enticing configurations. A thing of beauty, bright, clean, wonderful. One which sang.

Sound which dominated the ear as the glowing mist dominated the eye. As the subtle pulsing of it dominated the mind with its hypnotic spell.

"Don't look at it!" Dumarest forced himself to turn away, lifting a hand to cover Massak's eyes.

One the mercenary jerked away as he turned, snarling. "Don't look," snapped Dumarest. "Don't let it get to you."

"It's harmless. Just a cloud of brilliance. It shows me things."

"It's sucking your mind."

"No. That's stupid. It—"

"Damn you! Do as I say!" Dumarest lifted his hand, the fingers clenched, a fist which he poised to strike, then dropped as Lopakhin rose to his feet. "Tyner! Sit down! No, man! No!"

"Hilary!" The artist stepped toward the glowing radiance, hands extended, his face illuminated by something more than reflected light. "Hilary! My darling! You came back to me!"

"No!" Dumarest tried to rise and was thrown back against the wall by a sweep of the mercenary's arm. "Let me—"

"Stay put. There's nothing you can do. It's too late."

Lopakhin had closed the distance between himself and the shimmering cloud. He walked up to it, into it, froze as it closed around him.

"God!" Massak lifted his gun. "It's eating him!"

"Don't shoot!" Dumarest slammed down the weapon. "It's too late."

"I can give him an easy out."

"He doesn't need it. Look at his face."

It was calm, peaceful, the artist smiling a little as if he saw something which pleasured him. Smiling as his clothing dissolved into the mist, as his skin followed, the fat, the muscle and sinew, the bones and internal organs. Smiling still with bared teeth as his skull sat on the livid horror which had once been his body.

Then that too had vanished and there was only the mist which sang and pulsed and glided away down the facing tunnel to send murmurs and whispers of itself back in diminishing cadences.

"God!" Massak shook his head. "What the hell is it? A leech? A parasite of some kind? Why didn't it it take us all?"

"It had fed." Dumarest looked at the tunnel down which it had gone. "Lopakhin ran to it, remember. It didn't have to search."

But it would find them in its restless drifting, scenting them with alien organs, responding to the heat of their bodies, the electromagnetic activity of their brains. Or perhaps simply their bulk and composition, one different from rock. As were the things they had discarded. The debris which must have been left by others. All gone, cleared away, converted to basic energy to keep the thing alive.

"So we found it," said Mirza. "Or it found us. The thing I felt must be waiting. The guardian," she explained looking at them. "There's one in every legend. The monster which guards the treasure—but where the hell is it?"

"We'll find it," said Dumarest.

"When?"

"Soon." He looked at the casket, the flash of warning lights. It would have to be soon. "In a few hours, maybe."

Massak saw it first.

Chapter Fourteen

It was a bowl set in a cavern and centered by a column of lambent blue. Impressions fined as Dumarest studied it; the bowl was filled with a thinner mist the same color as the column, which was twenty feet high and half as large in diameter.

"It's like a fountain," said Massak. He stood in the opening from which he had discovered the column. "A fountain of mist, water, smoke—what the hell is it?"

Radiation made visible; energies trapped in a revealing medium which showed their writhing complexity as the beam of a flashlight was made to look solid in a dusty atmosphere. Forces which twisted, weaved, following a pattern impossible to grasp. Forming a substance which hovered between that of solid and gas. One alien in its fabrication.

It rested in a cavern shaped like the interior of an egg, the rock bearing a polished sheen. Stone shaped and worn by unknown years of attrition from the force it contained. The glow from it was caught, reflected, emphasized, enhanced by the near-mirror finish. The bowl formed a shallow pool, the edge resting ten feet from where they stood.

"We've found it!" The gun trembled in Massak's hands. "The thing Chenault dreamed of finding. The secret of Ryzam. Look at it, Earl! The source of renewed youth. Of health. Of life itself. You can feel it. Feel it!"

Dumarest inhaled, feeling the tingle coming from the column, hearing the soft susurration which could have been the rustle of breaking atoms. Material created, changed, recreated to form a continuous cycle of pulsing energy.

One which held the same hypnotic fascination as the shining predator.

"Wait!" Dumarest caught the mercenary's arm as he stepped toward the pool. "Let's check it out."

"What's there to check? We've found it."

"As others must have done. Where are they?" Dumarest looked around the chamber; it held two other openings, each, like the one they stood in, fashioned like a soaring arch. "We can walk around the pool and see what's behind those openings. You take the left and I'll go right."

210

He strode forward before Massak could argue, seeing him hesitate, then, shrugging, following his example. The opening gave on a passage with a peaked roof, the walls smooth and glowing with patches of brilliance. A twin to the one which had led them to the chamber. As he stepped back into it Dumarest saw Massak's arm waving in a signal.

"What is it?"

"Look." The mercenary pointed. "Another skeleton."

One traced in the smooth rock as had been the other, the only difference being in size. The first had been that of a mature woman. This was of a child.

"Barely three feet tall," said Massak. "How old would that make it, Earl? Ten? Twelve?" His tone hardened. "Who the hell would bring a child down here?"

"Maybe it was a midget."

"Like Baglioni?" Massak shook his head. "No, it was a child. Dying, maybe. Brought here to be cured. Then that shining thing caught it—and turned it into lines on a wall. One of those who never came back." He looked at the gun in his hands. "If I see it again I'm going to shoot. Don't try to stop me."

It would be like trying to kill the air but Dumarest didn't argue. "Let's get back to the others." He added, "Don't tell them about this."

The casket lay fifty yards from the opening at the junction of galleries, too narrow to permit of easy passage. Mirza sat with her back against a wall. Her skin was gray and she breathed through her open mouth. Toyanna was almost as exhausted and sat, crouched against the casket, her fingers busy on the keyboard. The red gleams of warning lights illuminated her face and hair with touches of false comfort.

"The power's gone," she said as Dumarest halted at her side. "The antigrav units are dead."

"It doesn't matter. We haven't far to go."

"You've found it?" Relief washed some of the fatigue from her face, her eyes. "Tama! You heard? We've found it!"

The surrogate at the end of its cable stirred, lifting its head, its hands. Self-powered it fed energy back through the wires to the pads transmitting Chenault's muscular impulses.

"How far?"

"Too far to carry the casket. We'll have to take you out."

"No!"

"And there's something else." Dumarest faced the surrogate as it rose to its feet. "You know what it is. Give me the coordinates."

"No. Not yet. Not until . . . until . . ." Chenault broke off, the surrogate jerking. "Must be sure that . . . that . . ."

Toyanna said, sharply. "We have no time to waste. Tama is dying."

And would die if left in the casket. A coffin which would hold more than the withered corpse of an old man. Dumarest looked at the surrogate, at the casket, at the machine again.

212

He said, harshly, "Listen to me, Chenault. I get the coordinates or I'll leave you to rot. I swear it."

"You can't!" Toyanna looked at his face and knew she was wrong. "Please, Earl, you mustn't!"

"It's his choice."

"Tell him!" Mirza had risen to her feet and now stumbled toward the surrogate. "Tell him, you fool! Tell him!"

"No."

"Then to hell with you." Dumarest turned. "Come on, Mirza, let me show you what we've found."

"What about Tama?"

"Forget him."

Dumarest heard the rustle of clothing, the scrape of feet, the touch of air compressed beneath a moving object. Warnings which triggered his instinctive reaction and he ducked, lunging to one side, dodging the swing of the metal hand which smashed into Mirza's face.

Sending her down to lie sprawled on the floor, blood streaming from her nose, her mouth, the empty socket of an eye.

Toyanna screamed, a shrill sound followed by Massak's roar of anger.

"You bastard! Earl! Watch him! He's gone crazy!"

He jumped to one side as the surrogate lunged toward him, gun lifting, finger poised on the trigger as he sought a clear field of fire. One blocked by the casket, the woman, Dumarest himself as he

213

dodged, weaving, ducking to avoid the murderous swings of the surrogate's fist.

"Chenault! Cut it out! Chenault!"

A man driven insane by his own stubbornness now finding an anodyne in action. To attack and destroy the man who had defied him. The obstacle in his way. A rage in which logic had no part.

And the surrogate was strong.

The proof lay on the floor and Dumarest had already experienced the strength of the artificial limbs. Then Chenault had intended no harm but now he meant to kill.

"Earl! Down!" Massak bared his teeth in a snarl of impatience. "Down!"

Fire blasted from the muzzle of his gun and a hail of bullets slammed into the massive torso of the surrogate. A natural error and one he corrected, swinging the gun to aim at the casket, lifting the barrel to rip apart the man it contained.

"No!" Toyanna threw herself forward. "No!"

A cry of protest drowned by the roar of the gun, the slamming impact of the bullets which churned her body to a broken, oozing ruin. A mistake; she had moved as the mercenary had closed his finger. As he went to fire again the surrogate was on him. Fist lifted, swinging down in a vicious arc.

One terminating at Massak's skull, breaking it open like a hammered nut, driving into the soft mass of the brain, causing it to spatter in a rain of red and gray particles.

Before the hand could be freed Dumarest was on the tall, grim figure.

To fight normally was to commit suicide and he took opportunity to leap on the machine's back, wrapping his legs around the thick waist, one hand reaching to probe at the eyes while the other lifted his knife and drove the point hard at the junction of neck and shoulder.

A gamble which failed; the blade slipping from buried metal to cut a gash in the artificial flesh. As an arm rose to grasp his neck Dumarest struck again, this time sending the point into an eye, feeling the plastic covering yield, the lens beneath shattering under the blow.

Half-blinded Chenault sent the extension of his body into a spinning whirl which threw Dumarest from his position to slam hard against the cabinet. That followed by a fist scraped against his head, tearing his scalp and filling his mouth with the taste of blood. A blow followed by another which he dodged, running toward the opening leading to the column of light, stumbling as his foot slipped on Toyanna's blood.

As he recovered his balance Chenault was on him, fists pounding, swinging like sledges to smash his ribs and lacerate his lungs with their broken ends. To fill his throat with blood and his eyes with blazing, darting flashes.

Dazed, Dumarest hit the edge of the opening, moved through it and, doubled, spitting blood, lurched toward the glowing light.

Chenault followed, the connecting cable unreeling from its spool with a thin humming sound. One which stopped as the surrogate came to the end of its lead, its momentum tearing the connection from its body.

It crashed to the ground, jerking, twitching as if the metal and plastic held a life of its own. Charged relays mimicking direct, human action. Responding to the power that was flooding into it from the column so that it looked like a helpless cripple striving to gain a safe refuge.

When, finally, it stilled Dumarest moved slowly back to where the casket rested. He felt weak, giddy and every move filled his chest with the pain of tearing knives. He was dying, drowning in his own blood, every breath accentuating the internal damage.

As he passed Mirza she groaned, lifting up a hand, her voice fogged with pain.

"Earl! Earl, help me!"

A plea he ignored, dropping to his knees beside the cabinet, fingers searching for the catch he had seen Toyanna use. A panel lifted to reveal a selection of drugs; measured doses in sting-ampoules. He selected two and drove the needles into his throat. The pain-killer acted almost instantly and he hoped the hormone-based cellular sealing compound was as effective. Emergency treatment but it enabled him to see clearly, to think free of pain, to select more drugs and to cross to where Mirza nursed her pain and fear.

"Here." He sent the sting deep into the artery of her throat. "That'll take care of the pain."

"I'm half blind. My eye—"

"Is ruined." He injected another dose of drugs

around the empty socket. "He knocked out the ball, pulped your nose and must have broken your cheek. The temple too, I think." He probed gently with his fingers. "Yes, I was right. Still hurt?"

"No, it's just numb." She sat upright and leaned against his supporting arm. "The others?"

"Dead."

"Chenault?"

"Hanging on." Dumarest glanced at the casket with its warning lights. "I misjudged him. I thought he'd yield when I threatened to leave him. Instead he went crazy."

"He was obsessed. He should have trusted you but—" She broke off, listening. "Earl?"

He had heard it too, a thin, high singing sound, accompanied by the ghost of bells. A sound they had heard before.

"It's coming back!" Mirza strained against his arm and climbed to her feet. "Earl! That shining thing! It's coming back!"

It came with the beauty of a drifting cloud, of light and brightness and of sad, sweet songs. Seeming to pause as it entered the space where the casket rested then to glow even brighter as it moved slowly forward. Watching it Dumarest felt his muscles grow tense even as his eyes drank in the alien beauty. It would be good just to sit and watch and let himself be absorbed by the glittering shape. To rest and cease from struggle and surrender to the inevitable. Death was a termination for him as for all things and where was the point in struggling

E. C. Tubb

when the final passing could be so enjoyable? To
die. To sleep. To let himself be enfolded in the
majestic pattern of nature. To become a part of the
shining thing as the food he ate became a part of
his own body and mind.

Then the shape he held against him slipped a
little and he stared at a dead, tormented face.

Toyanna, her body smashed to pulp, blood marring her clothing, her face, her hair. A doctor who
had tried to protect her patient and who had died in
the attempt. Had she loved Chenault? If so she
could still save him and others with him.

Dumarest rose, the body of the woman held
upright in his arms, her head lolling against his
chest. A weight he carried from behind the casket
to where the shining thing waited as if aware that
nothing living could resist its glowing beauty. To
hold it out before him, to press it against the
gleaming radiance, to feel it held as if by a multitude of tiny, invisible hands, then to release his
hold and step back and sag against the wall where
Mirza waited tense with expectant dread.

"God!" She closed her eye as if to shut out
what she had seen. The feeding which stripped a
victim layer by layer. One she had seen when
Lopakhin had died and had now seen again. "Earl,
will it come back?"

He listened to the dying cadences of its passage.
As before, when it had fed, it had moved on.
Satisfied with a willing victim, perhaps, following
some age-old pattern established on some alien

world. Speculations he set aside as, rising, he dragged the woman to her feet.

"I need your help. We've got to get Chenault out of the casket."

Touching her face, she said, bitterly, "Let the bastard rot!"

"Do as I say!" He was sharp; lifting the dead woman had filled his chest with the pain of new injuries. "I can't carry him, you'll have to do that. Hurry, now!"

He coughed and spat a stream of blood, feeling his lungs fill with more of his life's fluid as he tore open the casket. Mirza reached within, lifted the frail shape, brushed away the wired pads.

"You're a fool, Earl. If what you found can help you get to it. Forget Chenault. He deserves to die. In fact I think he's already dead. Leave him."

"I can't." Not while there remained the chance that the information he held could be gained. No matter how slender that chance might be. "Hand me those drugs."

They helped but not enough and Dumarest staggered as he led the way to the opening giving onto the column of light. It blazed brighter than he remembered, the soft susurration like voices calling from across vast distances, the tingle stronger now as if it were some form of atomic gas.

Mirza said, "That? Are we supposed to walk into that?"

"Have we any choice?" Again Dumarest vented a carmine stream. Fighting for breath he said, "It's a chance but what can we lose? We'd never get out in the condition we're in. Move, now. Carry Chenault into the column. I can't help."

"But you'll be able to manage?"

"Yes."

"To hell with Chenault. I'll drop him. Lean on me, Earl. We'll go in together."

"Just do as I say." *And hurry, woman! Hurry before the old man is dead and it's too late!* "Please, Mirza. Do it for me. Please!"

For a moment she stared at him and then she was gone, leaving him with the memory of her ruined face, the body of the old man held like a baby in her arms. Dumarest saw her step into the pool and walk without hesitation directly toward the central column. The mist-water-smoke-like blueness rose to her knees and, after she had reached halfway, he followed her as he had promised.

Slowly for he was heading into the unknown and every instinct warned him against it. The column could consume everything within it to atomic ash. Like the shining thing it could exist only to feed and yet it still was the only chance they had. One they couldn't afford to ignore.

Dumarest stepped into the pool.

Something like a tingling perfume rose around him and he inhaled, doubling to cough his pain as agony tore into his lungs. Sacrificing Toyanna's dead body had negated the healing medication and now even the pain killers had lost their power. He coughed again, staggering as the column spun in his sudden giddiness. One which dominated his actions, causing him to sag, to fall, to immerse himself in the pool as Mirza and her burden reached the column and vanished inside.

Too weak to move, Dumarest drifted like a dead fish in the lambent mist.

One which held magic.

The world was what a world should be with hard, clear seasons, a moon and stars a man could recognize and use to guide his way. A place where, at times, it was gentle and at others harsh. One where it was necessary to work and that was good, for to be idle was to grow weak. A planet which donated a heritage of pride.

"Earl!" The woman was tall with hair the color of flame, pendulous breasts above a belly swollen with child. She smiled and waved as he looked at her. "Take care of your son, Earl. I've enough to do teaching our daughter to cook."

A girl with a winsome face and hair the color of her mother's as the boy matched his father. The first-born who stood straight and strong and looked older than his years.

"I want to learn how to throw a knife," he said. "I have one, see? Mother doesn't want me to learn but I think I should. Please teach me."

"Why doesn't your mother want you to learn?"

"She thinks it will get me into trouble."

"Or out of it." Dumarest lifted the blade from his boot. "A knife is a tool, son, and only as dangerous as the man who uses it. With it you can cut, slice, chop, stab and throw. Like this." His hand moved, a blur as the knife was a blur, one which halted against the bole of a tree the sharp point buried deep.

"Like this?" The small hand rose, the knife it held spinning to fall far to one side of the tree. The eyes masked his disappointment. "I failed."

"You have yet to learn," corrected Dumarest. "Now, son, hold it like this." He placed the recovered blade firm on the palm and adjusted the fingers. "Hold it firm and make it a part of your arm. Now look at what you want to hit. *Look* at it. Forget the knife. Just concentrate on the target then, as if you're throwing out your hand, you throw the knife." He watched as, again, the blade fell to one side. "It takes practice."

"Lots of practice?"

"As much as it takes."

Dumarest smiled as he watched his son recover the blade, throw it, pick it up again with a dogged determination to succeed. It was good to have had the boy and extend himself into new generations and so ensure the continuation of his genes. Good to have a woman he loved and who loved him. Good for her to have children and to know that his love for her was big enough to encompass them all. Good to be home where Chenault—

Chenault?

Chapter Fifteen

Dumarest opened his eyes and frowned at the rock in front of him. Stone illuminated with a bright blue radiance on which he lay half-out of the mistlike pool. As if even in his sleep he had struggled to gain familiar ground and he climbed higher to draw his legs free of the pool and to lie, eyes narrowed against the brightness of the column.

One he had failed to reach but he felt no regret as he felt no pain. His only sadness was induced by the fading memory of a dream but the joy it had contained was something which still could be. Govinda was waiting with her warm, soft body and her wondrous scarlet hair. Kalin's hair but Govinda's talent could absorb the ghost of what had been and make it real again. And, soon now, he would be taking her home.

If Chenault was still alive.

A thought which sent him to his feet to stand as he examined his body. The pain had gone, the grate of broken, tearing bones. Beneath his fingers the ribs were whole again and strong. The breath he drew into his lungs brought exhilaration not agony. He felt no thirst, no hunger, no fatigue. The magic of the lambent pool had made him well.

Proof of the legend of Ryzam—if not renewed youth at least he had restored health. And the others?

The column was enigmatic, pulsing a little, flaring into a new brightness even as he watched. Flaring to fade a little as it followed the pattern of its nature. A pulse which must have been repeated many times as he lay drifting and dreaming in the pool. He had awakened naturally—if the others were still alive they would probably do the same.

Waiting, he did what had to be done.

The surrogate lay where it had fallen, a ghastly travesty of a man, too heavy for him to lift. Dumarest passed it, slowed as he neared the place where the casket had been left, slipped into it as he spotted no danger. The air stank of blood, Massak's corpse lying like a broken, headless doll in a dull brown puddle. Dumarest ignored it, uncoupling the cable from its junction, returning with it to the surrogate, looping it around the massive torso and then, sweating, dragged it to where Chenault had rested.

The casket yielded treasure; rods of heavy metal

and power packs now exhausted but still composed of compact atoms. Other things which he set aside then moved the surrogate to rest on the spread-out components. On it he placed the body of the dead mercenary.

At the opening, his hands filled with a wire-lashed bundle, he looked at what he had done. A funeral pyre lacking fuel but the composition was the same and, if the mercenary was watching, he would approve.

As a thin, high, familiar sound began to fill the air Dumarest hurried down to the chamber of light. The hollow egg, he was certain, would provide sanctuary from the shining thing. An assumption proved correct as the bell-chimes came no nearer, fading, to be lost in the soft susurration from the column.

One which, together with the varying intensity, cast a hypnotic spell almost impossible to resist.

Dumarest sat, his back against the wall, nails driven hard into his palms. To wait was never easy and now it was harder than at any other time he had known. Was Chenault alive? Would he emerge unscathed from the column? How long would it be?

Questions coupled to others and Dumarest retraced their path through the caverns a dozen times, mentally reviewing each turn and junction, each mark he had left, every danger they had faced.

Of them all the shining thing was the worst.

He rose finally, impatient to know the result of his calculated guess, moving softly back to where he had fashioned the mercenary's pyre. It had been without fuel—but now it glowed with fire.

With writhing movement and shimmering coruscations. With a covering of radiant beauty as the shining thing engulfed it, seeming more solid now, more inert. Condensing on itself, the writhings slowing even as Dumarest watched, the aura deepening, solidifying as if mist were turning to water and water to ice. A subtle change accompanied by a diminution in the bell-like singing. Down the bulk of the thing, in a line no thicker than a hair, a shadow slowly began to form.

One which widened as he watched. Growing darker as Dumarest turned and ran back to the chamber and the glowing column of light.

"Chenault!" His voice echoed from the curving walls. "Chenault! Mirza! Chenault!"

A flicker and the column was as before.

"Chenault! Can you hear me? Come out, damn you! Come out!" Dumarest stepped into the pool and headed toward the column. "It's time, man! Hurry! Hurry, I say!"

The column flickered again as, within it, something moved. A patch of darkness bearing the silhouette of a man. One who stepped from the column to stare at Dumarest with wide, clear eyes.

A stranger.

One tall, strong, dark-haired. A man of about twenty-five years with smooth skin and a generous mouth.

Looking at Dumarest he said, "Who are you?"

"Dumarest. Earl Dumarest. Chenault?"

"Yes." The man smiled, pleased at being known. "That's right. I'm Tama Chenault and my father owns the circus of Chen Wei. Where are we? What is this place?"

"The coordinates." Dumarest held out his hand as if to receive the precious figures. "Give me the coordinates."

"What coordinates? I don't know what you're talking about."

"The coordinates of Earth." Dumarest stared at the blank, uncomprehending face. "You swore you had them. You promised to give them to me. Damn you, Chenault! Keep your word or—"

"What word?" Chenault recoiled from what he saw in Dumarest's eyes, the knife lifted to hang poised before him. "I swear I don't know what you're talking about. I've never seen you before and I've never heard of Earth. But I've something else—see?"

He turned to reach within the column, turning again as he straightened to display the bundle in his arms. One which kicked and gurgled and stared with bright, shining eyes.

A naked baby girl—the red blotch of a tattoo bright on one wrist.

Captain Lauter reached for the decanter, poured, handed a glass to Dumarest before lifting his own.

"A wonderful achievement, Earl. I drink to it. The journey must have been incredible."

Dumarest looked at the glass; one mirrored to reflect the salon in bizarre configurations. His own

227

face was that of a stranger; warped, distorted, the thin lines of newly dressed wounds lying like lace on the taut flesh.

"Without the casket we could make faster time."

"But the perils?"

"I laid a trap for the shining thing; one of a huge amount of heavy metal together with Massak's body. As it absorbed the man it began to absorb the rest. I gambled on it being a reactive creature and the extra food triggered off its reproductive cycle. It became dormant as it condensed prior to splitting."

"Like an amoeba." Lauter nodded, understanding. "Which means there are more than one now. But the rest? The spiders?"

"We ran through the place where Hilary and Vosper died. I had taken rods from the casket and they made good weapons. Chenault managed to protect the baby."

While he had beaten off the swinging, gnashing, spined and feral insects. Looking at the lacerations on cheeks and neck the captain wondered how he had managed to save his eyes. The wounds on face and torso would heal but, inside, something would continue to bear the scars.

"And the rest?"

"We had suits—more than we needed. They yielded spare oxygen and other things. I rigged up a flame-thrower of sorts and used fire and smoke to get us to the surface."

Where luck had been with them. It had been dark and the flat creatures hugging the spires somnolent from lack of sunlight. Even so something had caught up with them as they reached the raft and, in the mirrored surface of the glass Dumarest saw, in memory, the bulk of it, the sting, the tearing, pincer-like jaws. A predator of the night which had died beneath the hammering impact of bullets from the gun he had left.

Then to where Baglioni waited and back to the ship and help and sanity. To the drugs which had eased the pain of injected venom. To dressings and sleep and now to satisfy Lauter's curiosity.

"How's the baby?"

"Govinda's taking care of her." Lauter refilled their glasses. "It's Mirza, right enough, the tattoo leaves no doubt. But how? How?"

"The legend," said Dumarest. "Youth restored— well, she got what she wanted."

"And so did Chenault. But she didn't want it in that way. She just wanted to be young and beautiful and get what she'd always wanted and never seemed to find. I guess you know what that was."

Dumarest nodded, thinking of the conversation they'd had in the caverns, the way she had touched his hand. A gesture which had betrayed her as had so many other small things when the facade she had built for protection cracked to reveal the true person it had shielded.

"She'll find it," he said. "She'll grow and, this time, she may know better than to believe that to be pretty is to be beautiful. That comes from within. And love can recognize it. It is the person which is important not the shell. Once she learns that, her life will be happy.''

As Chenault's would be; Lauter would look after their interests. And Mirza was free of the Cyclan—they would never look for their prey in the form of a baby.

Lauter said, thoughtfully, "What is it, Earl? "That thing in the caverns. What the hell is it?''

"A machine.''

"What?''

"I think it has to be a machine. Mirza said the area was unnatural and I agree with her. No natural force could have created it. Something must have come from outside, a ship of some kind, out of control and crashing with tremendous velocity. The impact broke the crust and its own internal forces molded the magma into the shapes we see. A long time ago, now, of course. A millennium at least. Maybe more.''

An accident which had ruined a world. One which must have seared the surface with flame and molten stone, turning metals into vapors, destroying all intelligent life. Only the insects would have had a chance to survive and their mutated descendants dominated Ryzam.

"The drive must have remained functional if only in part.'' Dumarest picked up his glass and drank and in the surface saw the lambent beauty of the glowing column. "The drive,'' he said. "It has to be that. One working on a different principle from our own. The Erhaft field cocoons us against the restrictions imposed by the speed of light but the alien mechanism works in the distortion of time.''

"A guess, Earl?"

"We can do nothing but guess but the evidence supports it. Look at Mirza and Chenault. Both entered the column old and both came out young."

"An intensification of the process which healed you."

"No. I stayed in the pool. In fact I must have crawled almost out of it fairly soon. The energies loose in the mist reshaped me. Maybe they were designed to do exactly that; to isolate the DNA blueprint and to shape the body back into what that blueprint said it should be. Another guess but it's good enough. The column was something else."

"Time reversal." Lauter frowned, nodding. "The tattoo on Mirza's wrist was recent; the flesh was still puffed. That makes her almost newborn. If Chenault hadn't picked her up—''

"She would have reverted to a blob of sperm. A zygote."

"Then nothing." Again the captain nodded. "No wonder those who found it never came back."

The column saw to that, luring them into its embrace, stripping away the unwanted years as it moved them back in time. Restoring the youth they craved—but as their bodies shed years of age so their brains shed the accumulated knowledge of those years.

"Chenault didn't recognize me," said Dumarest. "He didn't know me because, to him, we'd never met. I had to explain to him where we were and what we were doing. Luckily he was a quick learner."

Lauter said, looking at his glass, "Are you going back, Earl? Govinda—"

"No. It would be of no use. The pool doesn't cure and it can't help her. It can only restore you to what your blueprint tells it you should be. It can't take Baglioni and make him a normal-sized man. And the column can only make you young."

"Only? Men would give a fortune for that alone."

"Would they? Would you? Think about it. To be a boy again as you were before. A young man with it all to do again. The growing, the learning, the pain and frustration. The fear and hate and—" Dumarest broke off; not all had had a childhood like his. In a quieter tone he said, "It's a form of death, Captain. You retain nothing of what you know now. Nothing!"

"So much for legend." Lauter drank and reached for the decanter. "Join me, Earl, I insist." He waited until Dumarest set down his empty glass, then, pouring, said, "The treasure of Ryzam and it's something no one in their right mind would ever want to use. The pool, maybe, but any good hospital could do as much. And there's the danger— what was the shining thing?"

"Another guess," said Dumarest. "But I think it was a parasite of some kind. Vermin which managed to escape the destruction. Or it may even have been a cleaning device." He looked at his wine, red as the blood which had been shed in the pursuit of the unknown. Was Massak laughing at the joke? Vosper? The artist who had contained so much genius? The others? But they were dead and only the living held promise. "To the living," he said, and drank.

A toast in which Lauter joined. "So we face the future, Earl. Mirza and Chenault I can take care of but what about you?" He added, without waiting for an answer, "Mirza told me a little on the journey here. I'm not fond of the Cyclan and I'd like to help. I can take you to where you'd like to go. There are some nice worlds close to the Burdinnion; good climates, cheap land, plenty of space and no one asks too many questions. You could pick one. There's money; Mirza signed a note before she left the ship. Your reward for having helped her and I guess there's no doubt you've earned it." Lauter drained his glass and rose from the table. "Think about it," he urged. "Let me know what you decide."

Alone Dumarest drank his wine, then, refilled, lifted the glass and stared at the mirror surface. It seemed to hold more than the reflection of the salon and his own face. The dream was there and the disappointment. Chenault had reverted back to before he became interested in Earth and had learned the coordinates only when he was too weak to utilize them. Now the knowledge he'd held was lost as if it had never been.

Dumarest drank, the wine stinging with a bitter-sweetness, sliding like water down his throat to rest in his stomach.

A search of Chenault's study might reveal clues; but on Lychen the Cyclan would be waiting and would capture him within hours. A gamble with the odds set too high and the possible reward too vague. Another world then? A new place with new faces where, perhaps, he could find new clues? The search to continue until, like Chenault, he became too old to profit by anything he might find?

Had the dream been just a wishful longing instead of the certainty he had felt could materialize?

Need it be?

Govinda was real and here and she loved him as he loved her. Worlds, as Lauter had said, were plentiful and Mirza's gift would make life easy. There would be no children of her body but, given time, something could be arranged. A surrogate mother; his sperm and what could be salvaged from her genes. Not what she yearned for, nothing could ever be that, but as good as he could provide. And, if there were no children, no daughter who carried her mother's scarlet hair, no boy who wanted to model himself on his father, at least there would be peace.

Peace and love and an end to the obsession which had dominated his life. The search which had cost him so much and had yielded so little.

Earth!

In the mirrored glass he saw it, distorted as he was distorted, twisted, ravaged, suddenly hateful. An image which shattered beneath the closing pressure of his hand to leave the ruby of wine and scratches which yielded the carmine of blood.

A sacrifice to seal a bargain. One conducted by himself for himself with himself as the victim. Blood and wine and shattered crystal to seal his new resolve.

Outside the air was warm, perfumed from small tufts of flowers growing thickly around the ship. In the distance the spires of Ryzam loomed with somber menace, a picture in sharp contrast to that at the other side of the ship where the ground sloped to a stretch of sward soft beneath the foot and gentle to the eye.

"Earl!" Baglioni came running from the ship, his short legs pumping. "I wanted to talk to you," he said as he halted before Dumarest. "I had no chance before. You were all beat up and—" His hand made a vague gesture.

"I wanted to thank you for saving my life."

Dumarest said, dryly, "It's the other way around. If you hadn't waited we'd never have made it."

"And if I'd gone with Tama I'd be dead by now. Like the rest. A pity about Pia, I liked her."

"I know."

"And Lopakhin. Tyner was a genius."

"And Vosper was a good engineer." Dumarest, impatient to find Govinda, sensed the man was keeping him for some reason of his own. "But they're all dead now. Memories. Like Chenault."

"He's still alive."

"Not the man you knew." Dumarest hesitated, the midget and Chenault had been close. "Did he

E. C. Tubb

give you anything before we left? A paper? An envelope?''

"No."

"Are you sure?"

"He didn't leave the coordinates with me, Earl, if that's what you're asking. Maybe Lauter?''

Dumarest shook his head. Nothing had been left by Chenault with the captain. Nor with Baglioni—a hope that died like the rest and he wondered why he had asked the question. The search was over. He had made up his mind. Now and for always his future lay with the woman he had lost and found again.

"Govinda!" He waved as he saw her coming over the sward, Chenault following her, the baby in his arms. "Here! Govinda! Over here!"

The sun was in his eyes and she looked blurred as she came toward him, the glow subduing her hair a little, making subtle alterations to her shape. She seemed less mature than he remembered.

"Govinda!" He held out his hands to grasp her own, his fingers remaining empty as she ignored the gesture. "You remember that question you asked me once? Back in the valley? The one about would I ever leave you? Now I know the answer. I'll never leave you. We'll be together for always. Govinda?''

She wasn't looking at him, turning to face Chenault and the baby, her face no longer resembling the woman he had loved.

"Be careful, Tama! Don't hurt her!"

"Please!" Dumarest reached out to catch her

236

arm. "We must talk. About the future. Our future. We'll find a nice place on a good world and . . . and . . ."

She wasn't listening. She hadn't listened to a word. For her he had ceased to exist and now she had eyes only for Chenault and the baby in his arms. One she reached for to hold to her breast, crooning, her face radiant with an expression Dumarest had never seen her wear before.

"I'm sorry." Baglioni said softly at his side. "I wanted to tell you. It happened almost from the first—when you were being treated. She's found what she has always wanted."

A baby she could call her own. The oddity spawned by the power of Ryzam and which her mind could accept. The baby and the man who had shared its experience and so, to her, had become its father. The man who would now share her life.

Dumarest turned and walked back to the ship and the endless stars, the search which he would follow, for now there was nothing else.

Beyond the ship, traced against the sky, the spires of Ryzam signposted the graveyard of dreams.

Attention:

DAW COLLECTORS

Many readers of DAW Books have written requesting information on early titles and book numbers to assist in the collection of DAW editions since the first of our titles appeared in April 1972.

We have prepared a several-pages-long list of all DAW titles, giving their sequence numbers, original and current order numbers, and ISBN numbers. And of course the authors and book titles as well as reissues.

If you think that this list will be of help, you may have a copy by writing to the address below and enclosing one dollar to cover the handling and postage costs.

DAW BOOKS, INC. Dept. C
1633 Broadway
New York, N.Y. 10019

DAW

A GALAXY OF SCIENCE FICTION STARS!

LEE CORREY Manna	UE1896—$2.95
TIMOTHY ZAHN The Blackcollar	UE1959—$3.50
A.E. VAN VOGT Computerworld	UE1879—$2.50
COLLIN KAPP Search for the Sun	UE1858—$2.25
ROBERT TREBOR An XT Called Stanley	UE1865—$2.50
ANDRE NORTON Horn Crown	UE1635—$2.95
JACK VANCE The Face	UE1921—$2.50
E. C. TUBB Angado	UE1908—$2.50
KENNETH BULMER The Diamond Contessa	UE1853—$2.50
ROGER ZELAZNY Deus Irae	UE1887—$2.50
PHILIP K. DICK Ubik	UE1859—$2.50
DAVID J. LAKE Warlords of Xuma	UE1832—$2.50
CLIFFORD D. SIMAK Our Children's Children	UE1880—$2.50
M.A. FOSTER Transformer	UE1814—$2.50
GORDON R. DICKSON Mutants	UE1809—$2.95
BRIAN STABLEFORD The Gates of Eden	UE1801—$2.50
JOHN BRUNNER The Jagged Orbit	UE1917—$2.95
EDWARD LLEWELLYN Salvage and Destroy	UE1898—$2.95
PHILIP WYLIE The End of the Dream	UE1900—$2.25

DAW